IN TOO DEEP

A Shelby Belgarden Mystery

IN TOO DEEP

Valerie Sherrard

A BOARDWALK BOOK
A MEMBER OF THE DUNDURN GROUP
TORONTO · OXFORD

Copy-Editor: Andrea Pruss
Design: Jennifer Scott
Printer: Webcom

National Library of Canada Cataloguing in Publication Data

Sherrard, Valerie
 In too deep / Valerie Sherrard.

ISBN 1-55002-443-4

I. Title.

PS8587.H3867I5 2003   jC813'.6   C2003-901077-5   PZ7

1   2   3   4   5   07   06   05   04   03

THE CANADA COUNCIL | LE CONSEIL DES ARTS
FOR THE ARTS | DU CANADA
SINCE 1957 | DEPUIS 1957

Canada

ONTARIO ARTS COUNCIL
CONSEIL DES ARTS DE L'ONTARIO

We acknowledge the support of the **Canada Council for the Arts** and the **Ontario Arts Council** for our publishing program. We also acknowledge the financial support of the **Government of Canada** through the **Book Publishing Industry Development Program** and **The Association for the Export of Canadian Books**, and the **Government of Ontario** through the **Ontario Book Publishers Tax Credit** program, and the **Ontario Media Development Corporation's Ontario Book Initiative.**

Care has been taken to trace the ownership of copyright material used in this book. The author and the publisher welcome any information enabling them to rectify any references or credit in subsequent editions.

J. Kirk Howard, President

Printed and bound in Canada.⊛
Printed on recycled paper.
www.dundurn.com

Dundurn Press
8 Market Street
Suite 200
Toronto, Ontario, Canada
M5E 1M6

Dundurn Press
73 Lime Walk
Headington, Oxford,
England
OX3 7AD

Dundurn Press
2250 Military Road
Tonawanda NY
U.S.A. 14150

This book is dedicated to
Dylan, Michelle, and Bryan Sherrard,
who are loved more than words can say.

CHAPTER ONE

The first time I ever saw Amber Chapman she was pulling a long, red wagon that held a bulging plastic garbage bag. I knew right away she wasn't from Little River because she had on this weird outfit that made her look as though she bought her clothes in a second-hand store for the insane. Her jacket was badly worn green leather with a big yellow sunflower centered on the back of it and her pants billowed out in huge purple puffs that made it look like a long skirt at first glance. It was the strangest combination I'd ever seen.

There was something about her besides her unusual attire that caught my attention though, something in her manner of walking. Maybe it was the way she carried herself, her chin high and her eyes flashing dark darts as she made her way along Dylmer Street.

In any event, by the time I realized I was staring, she'd noticed me and stopped dead in her tracks.

"Do you have a problem?" Her gaze took me in, and I had the uncomfortable feeling that she was sizing me up and forming an opinion that was less than flattering.

"Nope," I answered as calmly as I could, although it was unnerving to stand there being appraised. "I just noticed you, you know, because I haven't seen you around before."

She didn't answer, nor did she turn away. Instead, she seemed to move toward me without actually taking a step, just leaning forward slightly and tilting her head up a bit.

"I'm Shelby Belgarden," I finally ventured. I offered a smile at the same time, but it wasn't returned.

"Well, good for you. I'm thrilled for you I'm sure," she replied haughtily.

"Has your family moved here recently?" Her attitude didn't exactly invite conversation, but there was something about her that made me keep talking.

"No, my family has not moved here recently." She spoke in short, clipped syllables, giving each word a peculiar sort of exaggeration. "I have moved here recently."

"By yourself?" I was astonished at the idea. She couldn't be more than fifteen.

"Not that it's any of your business, Shelby Belgarden, but yes, I moved here by myself."

"You live alone?" I couldn't help myself, even

though it was clear my questions weren't welcome.

"Did I say I was living alone?"

"Well, if you moved here by yourself ..." I trailed off, feeling confused.

"Maybe I came here to live with someone." Her hand rose in the air beside her and a finger poked toward me. "And maybe you should run along and bother someone else with your stupid interrogation."

"I was just trying to be friendly," I said lamely. It was no use. She turned away, picked up the handle of her wagon, and walked off without so much as glancing back. I couldn't help but notice that she managed to look dignified as she walked, in spite of her unusual attire and the fact that she was pulling along a kid's wagon.

It was unsettling, that's for sure. It wasn't so much her rudeness either; it was more the way she appeared to be so angry at the world that bothered me. I wondered what made her act that way and why she seemed so determined to be nasty.

When she'd almost disappeared from sight I headed over to my best friend Betts Thompson's house. I hadn't been planning to go there, but if anyone knew who the mysterious stranger was, Betts would.

Her face lit up when she opened the door and saw me standing there. That's one of my favourite things about Betts, the way she's always happy to see me. I can't remember ever feeling as though I was intruding when I've gone to her place unexpectedly.

"Hey, Shelb, come on in."

As we walked into the living room I saw books and papers spread out on the floor and asked her what she was doing.

"The biology assignment," she moaned. "My folks freaked over my last progress report. They told me if I don't bring my marks up I'm not getting anything for Easter."

In my house there's no such a thing as gifts for Easter. I'd get a chocolate bunny, and Mom still does an egg hunt even though I'm probably too old for that. Still, it's fun. But Betts always gets some really expensive presents. It's like Christmas all over again at her house.

It's the same thing with grading. A lot of kids get something from their parents for passing at the end of the school year, and Betts's gift is usually something really big. I asked my mom about it once.

"How come I don't get anything for grading?" I questioned casually at dinner one night.

"But you do, dear," Mom smiled. "You get to go into the next grade. You get a free education and an opportunity to do well for yourself and have any career you want."

Then there was some long, boring talk about kids in Third World countries who never even have the chance to read and write, and how privileged we are in Canada. I never brought it up again.

As Betts and I sat down in the muddle on the floor I couldn't help feeling sorry for her. She doesn't like school much and usually just does what she needs to do to get by. It looked as though those days had come to an end.

"I don't know how this all got into such a mess," she sighed. "I even found some of my biology notes in my math binder. It's going to take forever just to sort it all out and then I have to do those stupid charts."

I knew what she was talking about because I'd passed in the same assignment a couple of days earlier. The teacher had warned the class that anyone who was late was going to lose five marks for every day it was overdue.

"I'll help you get things organized," I offered. She perked up right away, and we set about putting her notes in order. As we worked I told her about my encounter with the oddly dressed girl.

But for once Betts wasn't up on the news. I could see that it pained her to tell me that she didn't know anything about the town's new arrival. Betts always knows everything that's going on, and I knew it was horrible for her to have to admit she was behind in such important gossip. I almost wished I hadn't mentioned it, because there was a good chance she would ditch her work and go off on a fact-finding expedition.

"Well, if she's in school we'll find out who she is soon enough," I pointed out.

"Maybe she's not, though. Maybe she got kicked out of school where she lived before and her parents sent her away to teach her a lesson."

Betts has a great imagination and can come up with a scenario to cover just about any situation. The problem with that is that sometimes she forgets the stories are her own inventions and the next thing you know they're being spread around as if they were facts.

"And maybe she'll be in class on Monday," I laughed, hoping that injecting another idea into the conversation would prevent her from going wild with her theory.

"Who can I call that might know?" The question wasn't really directed at me; it was the kind people ask out loud when they're talking to themselves. I couldn't help giggling at the intense look on her face.

"I swear, Betts, if you put as much effort into your schoolwork as you do in digging up gossip, you'd be a straight-A student," I told her.

She rolled her eyes. "I would, if it was half as interesting. Anyway, you sound like my mother now."

Accusing someone of sounding like a parent is a pretty heavy insult, but I knew she was only teasing. I finished helping her put her notes together and then said I had to get home.

My mother was in the kitchen basting a chicken for

dinner when I landed. There were potatoes and carrots on the table and I picked up a knife and started to give her a hand peeling. She likes it when I pitch in without being asked, and she always says thanks when I'm done. Today was no different, and it struck me that this is stuff she does every day of the week, but no one ever thanks *her* for doing it.

As we washed the vegetables I told her about the strange girl I'd met and how badly the conversation had gone between us.

"Sounds like she isn't a very happy person," Mom remarked.

I thought that was a funny way of putting it. I would have described the girl as mean or hateful. The idea that she was unhappy hadn't occurred to me at all. When I thought about it, though, it made sense. No one could be very happy if they acted that way.

I found it hard to concentrate on the book I was reading before bed that night. I kept picturing the flashing eyes and angry face and it distracted me from the words in front of me.

Well, Betts will know by tomorrow, I thought as I was drifting off to sleep. I guessed I could wait that long to find out something about the mysterious outsider.

I might have had more trouble sleeping if I'd known what was ahead, and how she was going to figure in the events that were coming.

CHAPTER TWO

It turned out that it wasn't necessary for Betts to fish for information because the halls at school were abuzz with talk about the new student. Having met her the day before, it came as no surprise to me that most of what was being said was negative. The main theme was that she was just plain weird.

When I saw her walking alone in the hallway the first thing that struck me was that her outfit was even more outrageous than the one she'd had on yesterday. She wore a skirt that looked for all the world as if it had been made by tying a bunch of scarves together, with triangles of different colours and designs hanging at varying lengths. Her top was tight blue denim with an assortment of buttons sewn on here and there. As bizarre as the ensemble was, I thought it looked kind of cool. Still, you can't get away with wearing something that's so different from everyone else at Little River High.

Whether she knew it or not, Amber had branded herself. From my brief encounter with her on Sunday, I figured she didn't really care.

"Her name's Amber Chapman," Betts told me, grabbing my arm in the hallway. "And she's staying with the Brodericks."

"You mean the gas station Brodericks?" I don't know why I asked that. The old couple who owned the gas station were the only folks in town with that name.

"Mmmmhmmm. I heard that she's the grand-daughter of Mrs. Broderick's sister, who married a foreigner and moved out west years ago. But that's all I could find out."

She seemed so disappointed not to have more news to share that I almost laughed. The only thing that held me back was knowing how seriously Betts takes the role of knowing other people's business. Some folks collect things, but Betts collects gossip.

It was hard to picture Amber living with the old couple. As sweet and tolerant as they are, they must have been as startled as the rest of us by her appearance and bad manners.

Aside from comments about her clothes, stories of her rudeness were spreading fast among the students at school. The few kids who had tried to talk to her had been rebuffed as quickly and thoroughly as I had been the day before. If being left alone was her game she was certainly going to be successful at it.

When lunchtime came it was obvious that everyone was waiting to see what she'd do when she got to the cafeteria. As soon as she got to the entrance a hush fell over the room. Most of the kids took quick peeks in her direction, but others, like Betts, were more overt about watching her and stared outright.

If she was aware of she stir she was causing, her face didn't show it. Except for the fact that her dark eyes scanned the room, she was so expressionless that she could have been a statue. Then she walked in and made her way directly to an empty table in the corner, looking neither left nor right as she walked. When she got there, she moved a chair around to the end of the table and sat with her back toward the rest of the room.

"Total nut case," Betts commented when she'd drawn her eyes back to our table.

"She's different all right," I couldn't help agreeing, even though I don't like to judge people. It was a lesson I'd learned recently, so maybe it hadn't completely taken hold.

"Perhaps she just marches to the beat of a different drummer." Greg Taylor slid into the chair across from me as he joined the conversation. My heart did a little jump, as it does whenever I see him lately. I'm hoping he'll ask me out someday soon. There was a time when he'd definitely been interested, but I'd done something that had changed that. I figured he'd come around in time, but for now we're just friends.

Betts rolled her eyes and unwrapped her sandwich. "Yeah, well, if she's going to be such a snob she can just march somewhere else."

"Maybe she's shy. Or scared."

"Tell him what happened yesterday, Shelby," Betts commanded. "That will open his eyes."

I filled him in on my meeting with Amber, leaving out the part where I was staring at her in the first place. He listened and nodded when I was through.

"Still, that doesn't prove that what we're seeing isn't just a defence of some sort."

"You're such a softie, Greg," Betts accused. "You just think the best of everyone."

"Shame on me then," he smiled. "I'll have to work on that."

"Did you get your assignment done?" I asked Betts, trying to change the subject. It was no use. She made a face that could have meant anything and then turned back to Greg.

"You're still working at Broderick's Gas Station, aren't you?"

I knew where she was going with it before he answered. Once he'd told her he did indeed still have a part-time job at Broderick's, she grabbed his arm and leaned toward him excitedly.

"Then you can find out why she's here! Ask old man Broderick the next time you're at work."

"I'd be glad to do that, Betts," he said pointedly, "if it was any of my business."

Her frustration showed as she tried to persuade him, but he didn't budge. I could have told her that she was wasting her time. Greg is an all around decent guy. There was no way he was going to start nosing into someone else's affairs.

Her badgering finally drove him away from the table, much to my annoyance. As soon as he'd finished eating he stood to leave. And then, to our astonishment, he walked right over to where Amber was sitting. We watched as he leaned over and spoke to her.

"Well, he'll change his tune after this," Betts muttered, never taking her eyes off them. "Wait until she tells him to get lost. It'll serve him right, too."

It looked very much as though that was exactly what was going to happen, at least at first. Amber turned to him with a scowl. Her face seemed to ask why he was bothering her when she'd made it so clear she didn't want anything to do with anyone.

But then the frown disappeared and she smiled! A few seconds later her head titled back and she was actually laughing. The next thing we knew, he was offering her his hand and she shook it. I figured he'd just introduced himself and she'd done the same.

"I don't believe it!" Betts sputtered.

We weren't the only ones who had witnessed it either. At least half the kids in the cafeteria were watching the unexpected exchange. I was sure that they were all wondering the same thing I was — what on earth had he said to her to make her change her attitude that fast?

I pushed the remainder of my lunch away, appetite completely gone. Greg and Amber talked for another minute or so and then he strolled casually through the room, paying no heed to the sudden burst of whispers. He didn't look in our direction as he walked into the hallway and turned toward the locker area.

Amber had resumed her position of leaning over her lunch with her back to everyone and her face down.

I guess I should have been happy that Greg had managed to break through her stony barrier. I should have been glad that she seemed to have made a friend in spite of the way she'd been acting. After all, she was new to the town and the school.

What I was actually feeling was nothing as noble as that. A sick feeling had crept into me, though I couldn't tell exactly where it started. It seemed to be partly in my stomach but it extended all the way up into my throat.

It would have been impossible not to notice that there was something very attractive about Amber, in spite of her odd manner of dressing. She had a little heart-shaped face with full lips and large brown eyes. Her dark hair, which she wore in a severely short style, made her look sophisticated and chic.

I was sure that Greg hadn't missed any of that either. And I had to admit that when she'd smiled at him, she'd been positively beautiful.

I suddenly felt very dowdy and plain.

CHAPTER THREE

The only comfort I had through the rest of the week was the thought that if Amber had warmed up to Greg, she'd eventually make other friends too. There was no sign that it was about to happen quickly, though, because she continued to keep to herself. A pattern was established where she'd take what we now all thought of as "her place" at the corner table of the cafeteria at noon and sit ignoring everyone. The only exception was when Greg stopped by for a few moments. She always seemed glad to see him, and they'd talk for a bit, but she never invited him to sit with her, which was a small consolation.

When he ate with Betts and me, she made a number of transparent attempts to drag information from him. He didn't bite and managed to steer the conversation away every time she tried to find out how he'd won Amber over or what they talked about.

I, too, was dying to know what he said to her during those brief exchanges, but I wasn't about to lower myself by asking him anything about it. Instead, I acted as unconcerned as could be, pretending that his growing friendship with Amber was of no consequence to me whatsoever.

Inside, I was tortured with the thought that he was quickly losing all interest in me, while at the same time his attraction to her seemed to be increasing. It's not as though I could do anything about it either. Her uniqueness was bound to appeal to someone like Greg, and I felt more and more dull and unappealing all the time.

It wasn't that he didn't act as nice and friendly toward me as ever. He did. But some undercurrent, or spark, between us seemed lost.

Then after school was let out on Friday, Amber paused as she was passing a group of us who were standing near the bus loading area.

"I'll see you tonight," she said to Greg.

"Right," he answered, giving her a smile that stabbed right into me. "Oh, and be sure to wear your best outfit."

She laughed, as though that was the wittiest thing she'd ever heard, told him she'd pick out something nice, and walked off.

Betts gave me a sympathetic look right away, which only made it worse. I hoped Greg hadn't noticed because the last thing I wanted was for him to know it bothered me. As unhappy as I was that he and Amber had a date for the evening, there was no way I intended to let him know I cared. After all, if he was no longer interested in me, there was nothing I could do about it. At least I could salvage my pride!

At that very moment, a commotion in the doorway of the school distracted me from my misery. Laura Peters was sobbing loudly while several of her friends surrounded her, offering comments that were meant to help.

"My mom is going to kill me," Laura lamented. "I'm not even supposed to bring it to school."

"It will turn up," a girl next to her said soothingly. Others murmured their assent, but Laura's distress seemed unaffected by their encouraging words.

We stood listening and watching as the little group moved toward us. Piecing together the ongoing bits of conversation, I gathered that Laura had worn an expensive watch to school, although apparently her mother had forbidden her to do so. She'd left the watch in her locker during gym class to make sure it didn't get damaged, but now it had disappeared. The worst part was that it had been the last gift she'd received from her grandmother, who had died the year before.

She'd reported the loss to the principal's office but was told the school could do little about it other than let her know if someone turned it in to the lost and found. It was her responsibility to keep her things locked up. She'd been advised to contact the police if she wanted them to investigate, but that would mean her parents would find out right away.

Of course, there was a combination lock on her locker, but by this point in the year a lot of kids knew each other's combinations. And it was common for us to yell them out to a friend who was going to the lockers, in order to save a trip there ourselves. It turned out that was exactly what Laura had done at lunch hour earlier in the day. Anyone could have remembered it and taken the watch.

I should mention that it's very unusual for anything to be stolen at Little River High. Not that everyone is totally honest and above doing such a thing, but in a small place like this it's just plain dumb to take something that belongs to someone else, especially something that you wear. You'd be caught the first time you put it on. Whoever had taken the watch wasn't going to be able to wear it without being found out.

It was pretty distressing to think that someone had gone into Laura's locker and taken her watch. I felt really sorry for her, not only for the loss, but for the trouble she was sure to get into at home because of it.

That, combined with the fact that Greg had a date with Amber that evening, put me in a dismal mood as I made my way home. It was only recently that I'd come to realize how much I really liked him, and the disappointment of knowing he'd fallen for someone else so easily hurt a lot.

Betts called me after dinner and asked if I wanted to come to her place for the night, but I made an excuse not to go. It was just one of those times when I felt like being alone.

Well, I guess the whole truth is I wanted to be alone to feel sorry for myself. I'd picked up some junk food on my way home from school and planned to lay on my bed, wallow in self-pity, and console myself with chocolate.

I turned on my CD player and put on some broken-hearted love songs, the kind you like to listen to when you feel that the people who wrote the sad lyrics are the only ones who have ever even come close to understanding how you feel. Except, of course, you know full well you feel worse than anyone in the whole world ever has.

So, my Friday evening was spent flopped on the bed, staring at the ceiling and singing along with the sad songs at the top of my voice. By the second song I was crying and almost enjoying it in a strange way.

I wondered if it was possible to die of a broken heart. Suppose I just lay there and expired from the sorrow — how would Greg feel then? He'd probably realize his horrible mistake and spend the rest of his life devoted to my memory, never dating anyone else again as long as he lived. He'd have to become a hermit and live alone in the woods, in a shrine he'd build in my honour.

I got a bit of satisfaction imagining that, but then it occurred to me that it wouldn't be much fun for me. Besides, I was checking carefully to see if there were any pains in my heart that might mean it was about to give out, and there was nothing.

Since my heart was apparently too strong to succumb to a pain even so great as this, I let myself drift off into a fantasy about how Amber would be really awful and disgusting on their date. I started imagining her at dinner, burping loudly, chewing with her mouth open, and other rather uncomplimentary things. I envisioned Greg's embarrassment and his sense of relief when the date was over and he knew he never had to see her again. He'd be begging me for a date after that!

That was more fun, but after a while I reminded myself that it was only fantasy. For all I knew they could be having the most wonderful date in history, fall in love, and get married some day.

I opened a second chocolate bar and put another mournful song on the stereo.

CHAPTER FOUR

It was raining when I got up on Saturday, which perfectly fit my plan for moping around the house all day. I meandered out to the kitchen, where Mom had just set a pan of bread to rise.

"Morning, dear," she said brightly, drying her hands on a tea towel.

"Morning," I mumbled without enthusiasm. It would be a real pain trying to maintain my gloom with Mom around. You know what parents are like. They can't just let you enjoy that kind of thing. Oh, no, they have to "get to the bottom of it" and then drive you insane trying to cheer you up.

"Did you not sleep well?"

"I slept okay."

"You seem a bit out of sorts." She looked at me closely, as if an explanation for my mood might be written on my face or something.

"I'm fine." I got a slice of whole wheat bread out of the bag and popped it into the toaster. "What kind of bread are you making?"

"Oatmeal brown bread. Are you sure you're all right?"

"I'm sure, Mom." I tried to keep from sounding impatient. "I just have a lot of homework this weekend and I was thinking about how long it's going to take to do it all."

That seemed to satisfy her for the moment, and it wasn't exactly a lie. I did have a lot of schoolwork to get done, though that wouldn't normally put me in a bad mood.

"Well, you can be excused from your chores today if you have that much to do."

I felt guilty right away. Mom and I usually go through the house and do all the floors and dusting on Saturday mornings. We launder the bedding too, but I knew she'd probably leave that until Monday since she likes to hang the sheets out for a really nice fresh smell.

"No, I have time to help around the house," I said quickly. "I can always finish my lessons tomorrow if I don't get everything done today."

She came over and gave me a hug and told me I was a good girl as I stood waiting for my toast to pop. That sort of irritated me too; I figure at my age I'm a bit too old to be referred to as a "good girl."

I wasn't hungry at all, especially after eating junk food the night before, but I sat down dutifully and ate my toast anyway. Mom would never let me get away without eating breakfast, and I guess there's sense to it. I remember her lecturing Betts about it one time, when she'd slept over and didn't want to eat in the morning. She said she never ate breakfast because she wanted to lose a few pounds.

Mom had launched into a big explanation about how if you don't eat in the morning your metabolism drops and your body doesn't burn calories efficiently all day because of it. She insisted that if Betts ate something sensible in the morning it would help her lose weight and that skipping meals could actually defeat the whole thing.

I'd been kind of embarrassed, the way I always am when my mom drags one of my friends into her "talks." Still, it turned out there was something to it. Betts had actually been really interested in what Mom was saying and started eating breakfast every day after that. The really weird thing was that she lost almost ten pounds over the next six months. Since that was the only change she'd made in her eating habits, it seemed Mom had been right.

Betts looked at her as something of an expert after that and often asked questions about nutrition and stuff, which, of course, pleased Mom to no end. She just adores an interested audience, and I don't always fit that description. But then it's hard to be attentive all the time since I'm pretty much at her mercy, a built-in guinea pig trapped in a perpetual lecture zone.

I cleaned up the kitchen after I'd eaten, moved everything off the counters and washed them down. I swept and mopped the floor too and greased the bread pans, since by then the dough was pushing up against the towel Mom had laid over top of it. I punched it down, formed it into loaves, and put them into the pans, covering them so the tops wouldn't dry out. I love the smell of baking bread and could hardly wait until it went into the oven.

I'd just finished my work in the kitchen when there was a knock at the door. When I opened it there was a young man there holding a long, white box.

"Shelby Belgarden," he said. I wondered how he knew my name, since I didn't recognize him at all.

"Uh huh," I answered.

"Oh, you're Shelby?"

Then I realized he'd been reading my name off a piece of paper stuck to the box. I nodded, confirming who I was for the second time, which seemed to satisfy him.

"Then these are for you." He passed the box over and asked me to sign a slip to show I'd received it. I thanked him and then we wished each other a nice day, the way you do to be polite to people you don't know. I guess no one really cares that much if the other person has a nice day or not, but it still seems the right thing to say.

Once he'd left I opened the box and was astonished to find a beautiful bouquet of pink and white carnations. For me!

"What's that, dear?" Mom must have heard me talking to someone and come to investigate.

"Flowers," I found myself smiling. "Someone sent me flowers."

"Why, they're lovely," Mom enthused. "Who are they from?"

"I don't know." I looked at the slip from the flower store, but there was no name on it.

"There should be a card in the box," she said.

Sure enough, I discovered a tiny white envelope with a card inside. I pulled it out eagerly and found the heading "Thinking of You" with a printed message underneath.

"From your secret admirer," I read aloud.

"Well, isn't that sweet! And romantic."

"But I still don't know who sent them!"

"I'm sure that whoever it was will make himself known soon enough," she smiled. "In the meantime, you can just enjoy the mystery."

I have to admit that the unexpected delivery changed the way I was feeling. It suddenly didn't seem all that appealing to wallow around in misery, and I found myself humming and happy as I finished my chores and got started on my homework.

Mom had found a vase for the flowers and I carried them from room to room as I went about my tasks. They smelled so nice, and I couldn't resist going over to admire them and inhale the scent often. It was the first time I'd ever received flowers, and it made me feel pretty special. There were ten in all, five pink and five white.

I spent a fair amount of time trying to figure out who might have sent them. It had to be one of the guys at school, but which one? If I had an admirer, he sure hadn't done anything to let me in on it.

A few possibilities came to mind, but I dismissed them all. The few guys who might be interested in me didn't seem the sorts to send flowers. If I'd received them a week ago, I'd have been sure they were from Greg, but since he had just started dating Amber I had to reluctantly rule him out.

Well, he'd be sorry when he saw that some other guy was madly in love with me and trying to sweep me off my feet by sending me flowers!

At dinner that evening Mom dropped a bomb on my happy thoughts by announcing that we were invited to the Taylors' place the next day. My folks have become friends with Greg's dad, Dr. Taylor, and we visit back and forth once in a while.

It was the worst possible timing, but I couldn't think of an excuse to avoid going there so I was pretty much trapped. The thought of listening to Greg talk about his new girlfriend was galling beyond description, and I dreaded the idea of having to smile and act as if I didn't care through it all.

Of course, I could always mention the flowers I'd received from a secret admirer. That perked me up a little, but mostly I felt confused by all the different emotions running amok inside of me.

CHAPTER FIVE

"Shelby, would you take this recipe over to Mrs. Carter? She's having company tomorrow and needs it before then."

We'd been getting ready to head over to the Taylors' place for dinner when the phone rang, and I'd held out a momentary hope that it was going to be Dr. Taylor calling to say he had to cancel for some reason. From Mom's request, I knew it had to have been Mrs. Carter asking for a recipe instead.

I took the paper she held out, slipped on my spring jacket, and headed out. Mom had explained that Mrs. Carter lived two streets away, in a green bungalow across from the bus stop. I had no trouble finding it and reached her place in a few minutes.

She ushered me inside despite my protests that I had to hurry back home, insisting that she had something she wanted to send back to my mother to thank her for all the trouble she'd gone to.

"It was no trouble," I pointed out. "All she had to do was copy out a recipe."

Ignoring my remark, Mrs. Carter disappeared into the other room, where I could hear her chattering on while I stood in the entrance feeling foolish. Her son Tony is my age, and I was afraid he was going to come along and think I was there to see him. He's a nice enough guy and all, but I never hang out with him.

"Here we are then," she said brightly when she finally returned. "This is chutney that I made last summer. You give it to your mother and tell her I appreciate her trouble, I do so. My grandmother, rest her soul, always made this preserve and it never fails. Why, my husband is crazy about it. I'm surprised we even have any left. I suppose that's because the boys don't care for it so much, although they love everything else I make, yes they do."

I took the jar from her, said thanks, and turned toward the door, but she wasn't finished. In fact, she went on so fast that it seemed she hardly had time to take a breath between words.

"You must know my boys, Raymond and Tony. Well, Raymond is older so you probably don't know him, but you and Tony must be close to the same age. What grade are you in? Tony is in tenth grade; would you be in his class?"

I told her I was in grade ten too, and that Tony was in two of my classes.

"Is that right?" she asked, as though she suspected I was lying. "Two classes? Only two? Now how does that work? When I was a student someone was either in your class or they weren't."

I explained that there were different students in each class, depending on the subjects each person was taking.

"Is that so? Well, well, I didn't know that. Tony doesn't tell me much about those things. He's away this weekend, gone over to Veander to spend a few days with his brother, Raymond, who's taking a course in computers at the community college there. The boys used to fight like cats and dogs, but they've gotten close in the last few months, and now Tony goes there every weekend he gets a chance. For goodness' sake! I just realized that he should be back on the bus any minute now. It's very handy, having the bus stop so nearby. Just walks across the street, he does. Why, maybe you'd like to come in and wait, and have a little visit with him when he gets home."

Half frantic to escape I blurted again that I really had to go, thanked her for the preserves, and rushed out the door before she could get going on some other subject. It struck me on the way home that Mrs. Carter could probably talk for a whole day without saying anything of much interest to anyone.

Most of the students who go on to the college in Veander after high school come home every weekend, since it's only about an hour's drive. I wondered if the fact that the Carter boys seemed to prefer spending time away instead of at home had anything to do with the fact that their mother prattles on that way. My mom talks a lot too, but at least she says something.

My folks were ready to leave for the Taylors' place when I got back home. I practised looking totally nonchalant in case Greg brought up the subject of Amber. Picturing myself being incredibly brave and saying things like "that's great" and "I'm really happy for you" (though I knew I wouldn't mean a word of it) cheered me a little. As long as I kept him from realizing how hurt I felt I could at least save my pride. It would be awful if he ever guessed just how miserable I was that he was dating someone else.

The house smelled great when Dr. Taylor welcomed us and ushered us into the sitting room. It made me hungry right away, even though I hadn't even been thinking about food beforehand.

Greg came into the room a moment later, and I was annoyed to feel the familiar lurch in my stomach as soon as I saw him. He smiled and came to sit in the armchair beside the couch where Mom and I were seated.

"Hey, Shelby."

"Hi, Greg. Something sure smells good."

"Probably my cologne," he joked, leaning toward me as if offering me a sniff.

"Oh, my mistake then, I thought it was your dad's cooking." I laughed in spite of myself, and it occurred to me that even if he was dating someone else, it was nice being his friend.

We all chatted for a bit, and then Dr. Taylor led us to the kitchen and took several large pans out of the oven. He'd made lasagna and garlic bread with a thick layer of melted cheese oozing over the top. A salad appeared from the fridge, and we settled down to eat.

It was scrumptious, and I'd have been tempted to take seconds if Greg, seated to my left, hadn't whispered to be sure to save room for dessert.

On top of being a good cook, Dr. Taylor is a great host. He has a knack for making guests feel comfortable and including everyone in the conversation. It popped into my head that some woman would be pretty lucky if he ever married again. But then, it wasn't that long since his wife had died, so he probably wasn't ready yet.

I'd drifted a bit from what was being said, engrossed in chewing the crusty-soft bread that seemed to melt in my mouth, and almost missed something important. It was such a passing remark that it was a few seconds before its meaning hit me, and even then I wasn't sure of what I'd heard. I leaned over to Greg.

"Did your dad just say you worked the last two nights?"

"That was my exciting weekend all right," he nodded. "Pumping gas and washing windshields. Why, are you jealous that your life isn't thrilling like mine?"

"But I thought …" I didn't finish the sentence, realizing that saying anything about his date with Amber would make it look like I cared. He must have been called in to work at the last minute and had to cancel. That pleased me, even though they had probably already rescheduled for another time.

"You thought what?"

"I just didn't know you worked on Friday evenings," I said, hoping it didn't sound too lame. The truth was, his schedule changed all the time, so my remark was pretty flimsy.

"I do sometimes," he stood to take our empty plates to the sink, "though I usually have either Friday or Saturday night off. But the Brodericks were away part of this weekend, so Amber and I worked all the shifts. They came back last night, or I'd have pulled another double today like I did yesterday."

"Amber is working at the gas station?" I could hardly believe it. Mostly, I felt this huge burst of happiness. Her comment to him hadn't had anything to do with a date! She was talking about seeing him at work. That also explained why she'd laughed when he told her to wear her best outfit.

"She's paying her room and board that way."

"I thought the Brodericks were her relatives."

"They are, but she doesn't want to freeload. The only way she was willing to come here was if they agreed she'd support herself by working for them."

I wanted to ask him why she was staying with them in the first place but didn't like to seem nosy. Maybe he'd let something slip about it later.

Dinner was over with soon, and Greg and I did the dishes. When we were finished we went to the book-filled den and sat chatting while the adults visited in the sitting room. It seemed that the evening passed faster than any I can remember, and it was with real reluctance that I got up to leave when Mom called me. Funny how I'd dreaded going there and then hated to leave.

We all thanked Greg's dad for the great dinner and the adults did their usual last-minute conversation thing in the doorway as we prepared to leave. I felt a stab of disappointment because Greg hadn't come along to say good night.

Then he appeared, coming through the kitchen, hiding something behind his back. When he reached the group congregated in the doorway he drew his hand around and held it out to me.

My mouth fell open as I saw that he was holding two carnations, one pink and one white.

"These should make up the rest of a dozen," he said softly, slipping them into my hand.

CHAPTER SIX

It was the perfect ending to the day. I told Greg the carnations were beautiful and thanked him, surprised to find my voice so calm seeing as how my heart was beating with excitement and happiness.

I could tell he wanted to kiss me, and I was a long way from being opposed to the idea myself, but since our parents were all standing around that was out of the question. On the drive home, drifting into one of my frequent daydreams, I pictured what our first kiss would be like.

Usually it's Mom who has a mysterious knack of knowing what's on my mind, but this time it was Dad who seemed to know exactly what I was thinking.

"I suppose," he said, glancing at me in the rearview mirror, "that this boy will be trying to put the lips to you one of these days."

"Dad!" I protested.

"What?" he pretended to be puzzled by my reaction. "I'm sure someone will want to kiss you sometime. After all, you're not that homely."

"Dad!"

"Well, you're not, dear. In fact, I think you're pretty passable, overall."

"Dad!"

He chuckled then, satisfied that he'd teased me enough for one day. Mom was amused too but kept her head tilted down and a little to the side so I couldn't quite see her smiling. The movement of her shoulders gave her away. Feeling pretty charitable, I forgave their enjoyment at my expense.

When we got home I added the two new flowers to the bouquet and sat them on the nightstand beside my bed. It hadn't even occurred to me that ten was a strange number of flowers to send anyone, and I made a mental note to pay more attention to details. It was that sort of thing that made for a good investigator.

Not that I think I'm some great sleuth or anything, but it was putting together the meaning of details that had enabled me to figure out who'd been setting fires in Little River only the month before. I wondered idly if I might be able to figure out who had stolen Laura's watch. I hadn't given it much thought over the weekend, being so immersed in the happenings in my own life. I pondered the matter as I fell asleep.

By the end of that week, though, Laura's watch was just the first of a number of things that had disappeared from students at Little River High.

It started on Tuesday when a CD walkman went missing from a bookbag that had been left unattended for a few moments. By Friday, the list of stolen items included small amounts of cash taken from a number of lockers, a Gameboy, a wallet, and a leather jacket.

The principal, Mr. Lower, made an announcement over the intercom, asking anyone who had information on the thefts to come forward. He promised anonymity, and possibly a reward, for those who did so.

No one seemed to know anything, and it was clear that the thief had been careful not to be seen. Everyone started being really careful, watching their belongings and changing locks on their locker doors.

The worst thing was that there was this air of suspicion all through the school. Anyone with an enemy found some reason to suggest that person was involved, which I thought was kind of stupid. Just because you don't like someone doesn't mean that person is a thief.

And then someone came up with a theory that grew and took on at life of its own in no time. It was impossible to trace the idea back to the original source, since it spread so fast that before long it was on the lips of half the students. It became so accepted that most kids looked on it as a fact by the time it had made its way through the school.

Amber Chapman was the only new student, coming to the school shortly after the March break. On top of that, the thefts had begun almost as soon as she'd arrived. I had to admit that it looked bad for her, but I'd already learned that things are not always the way they seem. Besides, aside from the coincidence of her arrival corresponding with the disappearances, there was no evidence to tie her into the thefts.

Even so, it wasn't long before she was looked at as the number one suspect, and a lot of the kids started giving her accusing looks. I figured she had to know what was being said about her, seeing as how a lot of the remarks that followed her around weren't exactly what you'd call whispers.

That was when I decided that I was going to try to find out who was responsible. If Amber was guilty, she deserved to be tried by the evidence, not by rumours and suspicions.

Greg was as aware of the talk as anyone else at school, and I discussed it with him one evening when we were talking on the phone.

"Since she insists on paying her room and board at the Brodericks' by working," he pointed out, "she doesn't seem the type to go around stealing."

"That's true," I agreed, "but then, she hasn't exactly endeared herself to the kids at school. It seems as if she hates everyone. Well, everyone except you. If she's taking things from the school it could be for personal reasons."

"Like what?"

"Well, something no one seems to know is why her family sent her here. One thing that's pretty clear, though, is that she doesn't want to be in Little River. Maybe she figures if she gets caught stealing she'll be kicked out of school. She could see it as a way to get back home."

"That's possible," Greg said slowly. "But if that's the case, it doesn't make sense that she's covering her tracks so carefully. Why wouldn't she leave clues that point back to her if she actually wants to get caught?"

I couldn't answer that, so I pointed out again that no one knew why Amber was in Little River. I suggested that maybe she was a kleptomaniac and that problems related to stealing could have made it necessary for her to leave her home and come here in the first place.

"There are lots of other possible reasons," he replied. "It's not fair to start guessing why she's here without any actual facts."

"You're the only friend she's made at school," I tried to sound casual, even though I knew he'd see that I was digging for information. "You must know something about her."

"Even if I did," he said firmly, "it would hardly be my place to go spreading it around. She has the same right to privacy as anyone else."

I couldn't help noticing that he hadn't actually denied that he knew something he wasn't telling. I almost blurted that he should be able to tell me because I was his girlfriend, but that wasn't exactly accurate. Even though he'd given me flowers, he hadn't asked me out, at least not yet.

Anyway, Greg isn't the type to gossip, and I knew it was just as unlikely that he'd betray a confidence whether I was officially his girlfriend or not.

Well, that didn't matter. A plan was formulating in my head. If Amber was guilty, I figured I knew how to catch her red-handed.

CHAPTER SEVEN

Well, I might not actually have been going out with Greg yet, but at least I had a date with him for Saturday evening. We'd just been leaving the school after classes on Friday when he sidled up to me, leaned over, and whispered in my ear.

"Say, Miss Belgarden, might I ask what your plans are for this weekend?"

"I hadn't really thought ..." I began in a normal tone of voice.

"Shhhhhh," he interrupted, sticking his finger over my mouth, "this mustn't get out."

I giggled and then nodded solemnly, forcing myself to look serious. "Sorry," I lowered my voice to match his. "What did you have in mind?"

"I can't say. But if you're free around seven o'clock tomorrow evening all will be revealed then."

"I think I can pencil you into my busy schedule," I hissed. "Where will I meet you?"

"I'll come for you, but you must tell no one of our plans."

"That shouldn't be much of a problem since I don't know what they are myself."

"Just as well. That way no one can torture you and make you talk."

I rolled my eyes. "Really, where are we going?"

"It is not time yet. You will know soon enough." He glanced around furtively as though to make sure no one was listening and then added, before heading off, "Remember, seven o'clock. Wait for the secret knock at your door."

I couldn't keep the smile off my face on the way home! All Friday evening I tossed ideas around of what he might have planned, but nothing seemed right. It certainly wasn't going to be something usual, like a movie and snack at the Scream Machine, our local soda shop and teen hangout.

To tell the truth, it was more fun *not* knowing where we were going. In a way, it reminded me of Christmas, and how much fun it is waiting and wondering what might appear under the tree. Betts told me one year that she'd found every hiding place and knew what her gifts were going to be ahead of time. I couldn't understand that at all. It seemed to me that she'd deliberately ruined the best part — the excitement and anticipation.

By Saturday afternoon my stomach was all a-flutter and the clock seemed to have slowed to a near stop. Every time I looked at it, willing the hours to pass, it had barely crept forward at all. I tried to keep busy, but it was impossible to concentrate on anything for more than a few minutes before thoughts of the date with Greg distracted me.

It's kind of hard to admit this, being fifteen and in grade ten and all, but I've never been kissed yet. Well, the truth is, I haven't actually done a lot of dating. The dance I went to with Greg last December was the only real date I'd ever had, and that wasn't what you'd call a smashing success.

Well, tonight that would all change. He was sure to kiss me, and I was ready! Goodness knows I've imagined it often enough. And, don't laugh, but I've practised a few times on my pillow and the mirror in my room. I guess that sounds pretty dumb. Betts and I got talking about that one time and she admitted she'd done the same thing, so maybe it's something other kids do too. I don't know.

Of course, Betts has been kissed so she doesn't have to pretend anymore. She got her first kiss from a guy named Jack, but she didn't even like him all that much. Betts told me it wasn't the way she'd expected it to be, which didn't surprise me at all. If you kiss someone that you don't really like, it's bound to be disappointing. I'd been waiting for the right person, and now that I'd found him, I was pretty sure it was going to be even better than I'd imagined.

I'd seen enough movies to know that you close your eyes when you're kissing, but suddenly a question popped into my head. Who makes the smacking sound at the end of a kiss? What if that was my job, and I didn't do it, and my first kiss ever turned into a disaster because it didn't have the right sound at the end? Or what if he was supposed to do it, and I did it too? It would be like a kiss with an echo. That would be even worse! I thought I'd better find out, so I called Betts to get some advice.

She wasn't home.

There's no one else from school whom I'd trust enough to ask a question like that. That's the kind of thing you only want to discuss with a really close friend, someone you know isn't going to laugh at you and tell everyone in the world.

Well, Mom was in the kitchen, and after tossing the idea back and forth and holding a huge argument with myself over whether or not I should ask her, I decided to go ahead. After all, the only things I had to worry about from her were raised eyebrows and a bit of teasing, which would be better than taking a chance that I'd mess up when the big moment came.

I wandered into the kitchen and plunked down on a chair, trying to look nonchalant.

Mom was glazing a ham, and there were potatoes on the table waiting to be peeled. I picked up the paring knife and started on them while I tried to figure out the best way to bring it up.

"Something on your mind, Shelby?"

I nearly dropped the knife. How Mom knows these things is beyond me, but it happens all the time. It's like she can read my mind, though of course that's impossible. Still, it's kind of scary the way she can take one glance at me and know that something's up.

"I was just curious about, uh," I hesitated, trying to find the right way to launch into the whole thing. She'd stopped what she was doing and was looking right at me.

"About kissing!" I blurted. I stared at the potato I was peeling as if it was the most interesting thing I'd seen all day.

"Kissing. I see. Well, what exactly were you curious about?"

"I was just wondering," I think I was trying too hard to sound casual, which was like wearing a flashing sign that would alert Mom that it was something important, "um, who makes the, you know, smacking sound?"

I waited for her to laugh, but she didn't. Instead, she came over and sat at the table with me and said, very solemnly, "Well, now, I've never thought about that, exactly, but it seems to me that it just happens on its own."

"Are you *sure*?" I was still worried.

"Yes, I think so. I think that's the way it is."

I was wondering why she didn't actually *know* when her face lit up, with that expression that tells you someone has just had an idea.

"Why, I'll get your father."

"You'll get her father for what? What has the child done this time?" Dad happened into the room just then and looked at me crossly. He's always going on that way, but it's only teasing.

"Oh, good, there you are, Randall. Come here and kiss me."

He looked startled but recovered right away and walked right over to Mom with a grin spreading across his face.

"Well, I don't mind if I do," he said, putting his arms around her.

"Gross!"

"Gross you say? I'll have you know that your mother is a darned fine kisser."

"You guys are disgusting!" But there was no point in protesting because they were kissing by then, right there in front of me. It seemed to last a lot longer than necessary too, if you want my opinion.

"Yes, I was right. It just happens on its own," Mom said brightly when it was finally over.

"Thanks a lot. I hope you know you've ruined my appetite for dinner."

"I'm sure you'll get over it, dear," Mom smiled, apparently unconcerned as to whether or not I'd ever be able to eat again.

"Whatever this experiment is about, I think it would be wise to do another test," Dad suggested.

I flounced out of the room while their laughter started up behind me. Honestly! You'd think they'd know better than that at their ages! After all, they're both over forty!

Thank goodness for the sanctuary of my room. I hurried there and shut the door tight behind me to block out the sounds of their nonsense. Then it occurred to me that I hadn't decided what to wear for the date tonight. I started going through my closet, taking out different things and trying them on as if I'd never worn them before and had no idea how they looked. I settled on my favourite jeans and a powder blue sweater.

By the time I'd laid out my outfit and put everything else back where it went, Mom was calling me for dinner. I joined them at the table, but my stomach was so nervous I could hardly eat. I was hoping they'd notice and think they were to blame, but if either one of them felt guilty it wasn't mentioned.

It was just after six o'clock when we'd finished doing the dishes and had the kitchen cleaned up. I went back to my room and was right in the middle of changing when there was a knock on my bedroom door. I knew it was Mom before she spoke, seeing as how Dad had gone off to help a friend of his who was having some car trouble.

"Shelby?" her voice sounded urgent.

"Yeah, Mom? I'm just getting changed."

"I'm afraid something has come up."

I pulled my sweater over my head and opened the door to see her standing there looking serious.

"I know you have plans this evening, but there's a bit of an emergency and you're going to have to help out."

I stared in disbelief as she continued.

"Julia has gone into labour and I have to take her to the hospital."

Julia and Paul Pernell and their two small children are neighbours of ours. I knew she was having another baby soon, but didn't understand why the onset of her labour should affect me. Mom cleared her throat.

"The baby wasn't due for another week and Paul is away. She's asked me if I'd sit with her until he gets back into town. I told her I'd stay with her, but that leaves her other kids."

And then she dropped the bomb.

"I'm afraid you're going to have to babysit them until I get back home."

Chapter Eight

I opened my mouth to tell Mom that there was *no way* I was giving up my date with Greg to babysit, but closed it again without making a sound. I knew very well there wasn't going to be any way out of it, and arguing would have been pointless.

If only it hadn't been the Pernell children, I might have been able to get a friend to take the job on short notice, but they're horribly shy of strangers. I've watched them before and I knew they'd set up a huge ruckus if they didn't know the person taking care of them. And their mother couldn't very well go off to the hospital with any peace of mind if they weren't with someone they knew.

"I have to call Greg and cancel our date," I said miserably. "Then I'll go right over."

"No, I'm bringing the children here." Mom's voice

was full of sympathy. "Maybe Greg would like to come over anyway, and babysit with you."

I was sure he'd love that all right! I'd just tell him to forget the great plans he'd made because we were going to do something even better.

I called his place, but his father told me he'd already left. That made me feel even worse because he'd have to turn around and go back home after walking all the way over.

The next half hour passed in a whirl as Mom rushed about, fetching the kids and hurrying off to take Mrs. Pernell to the hospital. They were both pretty agitated when they arrived.

"I want my mommy!" Cassie wailed. She's only four, but she's got lungs on her like you wouldn't believe.

Two-year-old Ryan whimpered beside her, holding onto her jacket with one hand and rubbing his nose with the other.

"Hey, we're going to have lots of fun," I promised, trying to distract them. I figured all the sudden commotion had probably upset them.

I dug out some colouring books and crayons and set them up at the table. They didn't budge. There were tears starting down Cassie's face, and Ryan's blubbering was sure to make them a matched set any second.

"Hey, want some cookies?"

"I want *Mommy*. I want to go home."

"I have to go," Ryan chimed in.

"You can't go right now," I was getting exasperated. "Mommy will be back soon and then you can go home." That wasn't exactly true, but I'd have said almost anything at that point.

Ryan joined his sister by bursting into full-fledged howling then. A few seconds later I realized that when he'd said he had to go, he hadn't meant home. A wet patch darkened the crotch of his pants, spreading down both legs. He sobbed louder.

"Ryan wet his pants," Cassie paused just long enough to point this out and then resumed crying.

"Hello there."

I spun around to see Greg standing in the open doorway.

"I knocked, but no one came. Then I heard the commotion and I thought I'd better open the door or you'd never know I was here. I hope that was okay."

"Oh, Greg! I'm so sorry. I tried to call but you'd already left. I can't go out tonight." I quickly explained what had happened, though it wasn't easy being heard over the din. It's amazing how much noise two small children can make!

"The little fellow wet himself," Greg whispered when I'd finished.

"Yes, I know. It happened just before you came in."
I turned back to Cassie and Ryan. "Please stop crying,"
I begged ineffectively.

"Can I help?"

"Thanks, but they don't like strangers."

"Forgive me for pointing this out, but they don't
seem all that fond of you either." He took a few steps
toward them and squatted down.

The phone rang and I picked it up, covering my
other ear so I could hear the caller. It was Betts.

"Hey, Shelb! Mom said you phoned earlier."

"Yeah." That had been the call to ask her the kiss
question, but I wasn't about to tell her that with Greg
right there. "I was just calling to chat."

"*What* is that racket at your place?"

I gave her the condensed version.

"Gee, stuck with bawling ankle-biters on a Saturday
night. That sucks. Anyway, I thought you had a date
with Greg."

"Yeah, well, so much for that. Someone should
have mentioned it to Mrs. Pernell. Maybe she could
have held off a bit."

"I wish I could help, but I'm going to the show
with Derek."

I sort of doubted that Betts was wishing with all her
heart that she could take my place, but I thanked her
just the same and then said goodbye. When I turned

back to the kids I was astonished to see Greg helping Cassie out of her jacket. She was still sniffling but the full-blown crying had stopped. Ryan's sobs seemed to be diminishing too. Greg glanced up at me.

"I'm just trying to figure out if, uh," he paused.

"Cassie," I prompted.

"Yes, if Cassie here is an angel or a princess. And I see we have our answer. Since there are no wings, she must be a princess."

"Yeah, she's a princess all right." I tried to hide the sarcasm.

"Princesses need princess crowns for their heads," he told her. "We'd better get your maidservant on that right away. Shelby?"

"A crown it is," I smiled. "What colour crown would you like?"

"Pink," she hiccupped.

"Don't forget the jewels," Greg said solemnly. "And now, young prince ..."

"Ryan."

"Indeed. Young Prince Ryan and I are going to see if there are any dragons in your bathtub. Would there be a change of royal clothes around here anywhere?"

Ryan's eyes got bigger at the mention of dragons. I passed Greg the bag Mom had brought along with their pyjamas in it and they went off to search for mythical creatures in the bathroom.

Cassie and I had almost finished creating her crown out of construction paper when the two males returned. Ryan was riding on Greg's shoulders, but he clamoured to get down.

"Me too, Sir Greg," he commanded.

"A crown for Prince Ryan, fair damsel!" Greg swung the tyke off his shoulders and onto a chair.

"How did it work out that you got to be Sir Greg and I got to be a maidservant?"

"Silence! Sir Greg is special assistant to the prince."

We all worked together, cutting and pasting until two crowns suitable for our wee royalty were finished. Greg had the kids laughing most of the time with his antics.

Watching him, I felt something swell up in my heart. It nearly made me cry, but not in a bad way.

Everything was royal, though Ryan pronounced it "oil." There were royal cookies and royal milk and royal facecloths to wash the royal faces after they'd eaten.

"They caught on pretty fast," I hissed to Greg as I carried Cassie on my shoulders. It seemed that they'd both decided their royal feet were too tired to walk. "If you ask me, you've turned them into royal pains with all these royal demands."

"Apparently you haven't yet learned your place," he whispered back. "A good maidservant does her mistress's bidding happily." He sighed and frowned. "I'm afraid you're going to have to be sent to the dungeon if this complaining continues."

The truth was, I'd never had so much fun babysitting. I could hardly believe it when Greg mentioned that it was almost nine-thirty and wondered aloud about the royal bedtime.

"I don't wanna go to bed!" Princess Cassie objected.

"Well, we must consult the royal bedtime bowl then," Greg said quickly. "The magic bowl will tell us if your majesties are tired or not."

"I'm *not* tired." But the word "magic" had her attention.

"Sir Greg requires vinegar and soda for the magic potion," he told me.

I fetched them, wondering what he was up to. He poured a little vinegar into a bowl and sat it on the middle of the table.

"The magic bowl knows all things," he told the wide-eyed children. "We must add the magic powder and the bowl will tell us what is to be done. If it bubbles, that means you must have a royal story in bed. If it doesn't, you must go right to sleep."

They watched breathlessly as he spooned a little baking soda into the bowl. Of course it fizzled and bubbled like crazy.

"Aha! The bowl says you get a story!"

They clapped and followed him into the spare

room, insisting that he lay between them on the double bed. I ran for a storybook, returning with an old favourite from when I was a child.

"Dr. Seuss, *The Sneetches*!" Greg nodded approvingly. "I love this story."

He'd only finished about half of it before they were fast asleep. Extracting himself from the pair, he brought the book along to the living room and motioned me to sit on the couch.

"You deserve to hear the rest of this, seeing as how you've been a pretty good maidservant after all." He sat close beside me and continued the story.

"You were great," I told him when he'd finished.

"Thank you. I've been practising my reading."

"Not that! I mean with the kids and everything. I don't think too many guys would have done what you did, especially when you'd made plans and all."

"It was all for the best anyway," he said, "did you notice that it's raining?"

I hadn't, but he was right. It was raining. "Were we going to be doing something outside?" I asked.

"Maybe." He smiled teasingly. "But *you* won't know until we can reschedule."

And then — I'm almost positive he was going to lean over and kiss me. I say "was" because at that moment headlights shone in the window as a car pulled into the driveway.

It was Dad. He was surprised to find us there, and I explained about Mrs. Pernell and everything.

"Well, that's too bad. I'll give you a lift home, so you don't have to walk in the rain, Greg." Dad offered.

And the next thing I knew Greg was saying good night and getting in the car.

Why, oh why, couldn't Dad have come home ten minutes later? I was starting to think I was jinxed.

By the end of the next week, that feeling was going to be a lot stronger!

CHAPTER NINE

By Monday, things were back to normal at our house. Mr. Pernell picked Cassie and Ryan up and took them home on Sunday evening after reporting that his wife had safely delivered a new baby boy. He thanked us profusely for all we'd done and tried to pay me for babysitting the evening before.

I knew Mom wouldn't want me to take money since it had been an emergency, so I told him I'd like it if he'd just buy the new baby something with it instead. He said I was a wonderful girl and promised they were going to call me any time they needed a sitter from then on. I wasn't what you'd call thrilled but I tried to act enthused at the idea. Just the *thought* of having to cart those two around *and* take care of a new royal Pernell was enough to exhaust me. After all, it's not as though Greg would be there to help.

I'll tell you one thing — I'm not having children before I'm at least twenty-five. I've known a few girls who had babies while they were still in school, and I don't think they had any idea what they were getting into. Taking care of kids is hard work, and it's not like you just put in a shift and go home. You're in it full time, twenty-four-seven, with no days off — ever! And babies! I've babysat a few of them, and it's enough to send a person off the deep end when they cry and you can't get them to stop.

Anyway, after all the chaos, I was actually looking forward to going back to school by the time the weekend was over. The first thing that I heard when I got to class was that there had been yet another theft. It seemed it had happened on Friday, but it wasn't discovered until that morning, when a grade twelve student named Jeremy went to his locker and found that the money he'd kept there was gone. It was no small amount either, almost two hundred dollars in all. He'd been collecting for the walk-a-thon we hold every year to sponsor a child for summer camp. Jeremy was the one who'd organized the whole thing this year because it was one of those student initiatives that counts as a credit in the entrepreneur class.

He reported it to the office right away, and if you think the students were upset before, you should have seen them that day. The idea that anyone would take money that was meant for an underprivileged kid was enough to enrage the whole student body.

The new theft reminded me of my plan to catch Amber, if she was guilty. And it was looking more and more as if she probably was. Someone had noticed that morning that she was wearing a brand new pair of air runners, the kind that cost at least a hundred and fifty bucks. Suspicion toward her was growing by the minute. Of course, no one accused her to her face, but it was in the air like a low, dark fog.

It was the kind of plan that has to wait for an opportunity, and I was watching. On Tuesday, just before classes, I got my chance.

Amber had gone into the girls' washroom, and I followed her in a moment later. Bending down, I saw that there was only one stall occupied, so I knew that we were the only two people in there. I slipped my watch off and laid it by the sink and then stepped quickly into a stall. I closed the door but didn't lock it and stood watching through the crack.

A moment later she came out and went to the sink to wash her hands. I breathed quietly, hoping she'd notice the watch, which was at the sink next to the one where she stood. Sure enough, I saw her glance over and then stop and stare at the watch. Then she was drying her hands, still looking where it sat shining under the lights. The next moment, after a slight pause, she went back to the sink and picked it up. She glanced to the left and right, as if to make sure no one was watching, and slipped it into her pocket.

I'd done it! I'd caught the thief! My heart was pounding hard and I realized that I'd been holding my breath. The sudden expulsion of air from my lungs, followed by a huge gasp, seemed loud enough to be heard right out into the corridor, and I was sure she must have heard me. I expected her to turn and find me there, but she just kept walking and a second later was out the door.

I raced out of the bathroom and caught up with Amber just before she turned the corner.

"I saw you. I caught you red-handed," I told her angrily. "Now I'm going to the principal, and you might as well come with me."

She stood very still, her face strangely expressionless. Then she shrugged indifferently, nodded, and walked with me to the office.

A moment later Mr. Lower ushered us into his inner office and motioned us to seat ourselves in the chairs across from his desk.

"What's this all about then?"

I blurted out my story, uncomfortably aware that Amber was sitting straight up in her chair and looking at me the entire time I spoke. When I'd finished, Mr. Lower turned to her.

"Well, Amber? What do you have to say about this?"

"I wasn't *stealing* the watch," she told him calmly. "I saw it lying by the sink and I thought someone left it there by mistake. I was going to turn it in." She reached into her pocket, drew out the watch, and plunked it on his desk.

Of course, what else could she say? She was hardly going to admit that she was a thief.

"You heard what Amber said, Shelby."

I could hardly believe my ears! Here I was, presenting him with the cause of all the recent trouble in the school, and he was acting as if I should just take her word for it.

"I heard her all right," I acknowledged. "I just don't believe her."

"I see. Well, Amber, I'd like to talk to Shelby in private. You can return to your class now."

She got up and walked deliberately past me, and as she did a flicker of a smile crossed her lips. The smug look on her face made me so furious I could hardly think straight.

When she'd gone, Mr. Lower cleared his throat and spoke to me again.

"Let me ask you something, Shelby. What would you do if you went into the girls' room and saw a watch sitting by the sink?"

"What do you mean?" I stammered.

"Just what I said. What would you have done if you'd found the watch?"

"I'd have brought it to the office." I felt my face getting warm as I answered.

"That's exactly what Amber stated she was going to do."

"But how do you know she's telling the truth?"

"How do *you* know she's not?"

"But we've had all these thefts!" I pointed out.

"Yes, we have. And that means we must be extra careful. A person's reputation is at stake here. It would be unfair to make accusations unless we're very, very sure. Do you understand?"

"Yes," I said, pushing down my anger. There was obviously no point in trying to talk to him. "I understand."

I understood all right. I understood that she was getting away with it … this time.

Chapter Ten

It made me seethe every time I so much as laid eyes on Amber the rest of the week. She moved through the school with her usual air of studied indifference, continuing to act as though none of the gossip affected her in the least. It was impossible that she didn't hear the things being said about her, although I refrained from adding my own bit of information to the rumours that were already flying.

It was tempting to tell Betts and Greg what had happened in the washroom, but I didn't. I'd considered sharing the details of my trap with them but decided against it because it would have been embarrassing to have to recount the scene in Mr. Lower's office. I thought it would be better to wait until I had her solid. If only I'd said something I might have avoided what happened later.

There were a few more minor items that disappeared through the week, but everyone was being a lot more cautious about leaving anything of value in their lockers. There were a couple of comical things that happened too, which were surely brought on by the growing paranoia in the school.

The first was when Christine Falconer thought someone had taken her eyeglasses. She set up quite a stir, yelling that she was going to kill whoever had done it and sobbing that her mother was going to be furious about having to buy another pair, since those ones were new and had been expensive.

"What good would your glasses be to anyone else?" someone nearby asked. I thought it was a pretty sensible question, but it only sent Christine into further fits of railing against the supposed culprit.

Anyway, it turned out that she'd left her glasses on the desk in her last class. This discovery ended her death threats and sobs and replaced them with a dark red blush that wasn't helped by the hoots of laughter from the students who'd witnessed the whole thing.

The other incident was the same day, and it involved Tony Carter, the kid whose mother had trapped me with her longwinded chatter when I'd taken a recipe there. He positively freaked when he went to his locker and couldn't find the deck of cards he kept there. Tony does card tricks in the lunchroom sometimes, and they're pretty good too. He'd get you to pick a card out of the deck and then he'd tell you what it was before it was turned over. I don't know how he did it, but he was right every time. When he first started out, he'd get dollar bets on the trick, but since he always won it wasn't long before no one would bet with him anymore.

So there he was, just ranting and raving that his lucky deck was missing. As if anyone would want an old deck of cards! Betts told me about it, since she'd been nearby when it happened.

"You should have seen him!" she giggled. "His face was practically purple, he was so upset. He tore his whole locker apart trying to find those stupid cards, throwing everything out on the floor and going on like a madman."

I bit into my sandwich as she continued, all the while keeping an eye out for Greg. He was late coming to lunch that day, and since he hadn't yet mentioned anything about getting together this weekend I was really anxious to see him. It was already Thursday, so if he intended to ask me to do something with him it would have to be soon.

"I swear," Betts went on with her story, "he was about to cry. Why on earth anyone would get into such a panic over a deck of cards is beyond me, but he was in an awful state. And then they slid out from the middle of a notebook while he was kicking his stuff in a rage and he just fell to his knees and grabbed them and — I'm not making this up — he actually kissed them!"

I laughed at the thought of that and Betts looked satisfied, the way she does when she's told a particularly juicy story. But at the same time I couldn't help thinking it was pretty sad that the thefts at school had caused such a horrible reaction among the students. We never used to have to worry about our things being stolen, and it was creating a tension that affected everyone.

Greg came along then, and to my delight he asked me right away if I was interested in making plans on Friday evening. I asked him what he had in mind, as if that would affect my decision. If he'd suggested that we sit in a farmer's damp field and watch a cow chew its cud I'd have been game.

"Come to my place for dinner, and then we'll figure out what we're going to do for the rest of the evening."

I agreed happily, though I was a bit disappointed that we apparently weren't going to do whatever it was he'd had planned last Saturday. But then, maybe he was going to surprise me with that after dinner.

There was a surprise that night all right, but it wasn't what I was expecting! I got there at quarter to five and sat in the kitchen while Greg and his dad chopped vegetables for dinner.

"I hope you like stir-fry, Shelby."

I assured Dr. Taylor that I did and offered to help, but he told me they had everything under control. That made me smile because I got picturing the vegetables getting unruly and needing to be subdued. Then I felt stupid for sitting there with a big grin on my face when no one else in the room knew why. If they noticed, though, they didn't mention it, and at least I didn't laugh out loud. That's happened more than a few times, when something has struck me funny. It's usually in a situation that's serious too, which has caused me problems more than once.

The absolute worst is when that happens in church. It's not as if you can just up and laugh in the middle of a sermon, and I don't mean to be irreverent or anything, but sometimes I'll get a thought that strikes me as hilarious. The best I can do under those circumstances is try to act as if I'm taken in a sudden fit of coughing, but even that draws cross looks from my mother.

And once, about a year ago, we were visiting my Great-Aunt Isabel and were sitting in her parlour. Well, she calls it a parlour, but if you ask me it's just a stuffy, depressing room where adults discuss really boring things.

Anyway, my great-aunt was looking especially severe, seated in the chair she always occupies in that room. I never fail to get the feeling that she thinks she's holding court, like some queen reigning over her loyal subjects. She talks in clipped syllables and looks down her nose at you in a way that makes you sure she's finding fault with what she sees. It annoys her when other people try to have a fair share in the conversation too. She'll give them a look as if she can't quite believe their audacity in thinking *they* have something worth listening to when she, Queen Isabel, is there.

So, this particular day we were gathered in the parlour and being subjected to Aunt Isabel's longwinded talk, which was mostly about herself. It seems that's the topic that interests her most, and it centres primarily around her health. She proudly claims a lengthy list of ailments that all seem to end in "itis," like arthritis and bursitis and the like.

And then she mentioned her husband, who passed away about twenty years ago. There's a picture of the two of them when they were young on the wall in a fancy oval frame, and you can see, even though it's a bit fuzzy, that he has the look of a man who's trapped.

"My late husband," Aunt Isabel started to say, and then broke off when I burst out laughing. You see, it had just hit me that he was *really* late, late by a good twenty years, and that if she was what he had to come home to every day, I didn't blame him a bit.

Well, you can just imagine the looks I got. Mom nearly glared me into stopping, but then I caught Dad's eye and it seemed there was a twinkle there, which sent me into another fit of laughter.

Aunt Isabel cleared her throat, as if to regain command of the room, and gave me a haughty look. I pulled myself together and said I was sorry, which I wasn't.

"It seems you find something amusing about this, Miss Shelby. Perhaps you'd like to explain your merriment to the rest of us."

I mumbled something incoherent about suddenly remembering a funny incident that had happened at school, and after a few more withering glances at me, Aunt Isabel went back to her story. I figured I was in for a big lecture on the way home, and Mom didn't disappoint me.

Drawing my thoughts back to the present I saw that Greg and his dad were finished chopping the vegetables. Dr. Taylor got an electric wok out of the cupboard and had just plugged it in when there was a knock at the door.

"There's our other guest," Greg said, which was news to me. Before I had time to wonder who else was coming, he'd reached the door and swung it open.

To my complete shock and horror, there stood Amber Chapman!

CHAPTER ELEVEN

It was clear that Amber hadn't expected to see me any more than I'd expected to see her. She was visibly startled, which gave me some satisfaction despite my dismay at seeing her in the doorway. It was the first time I'd seen her in the least bit ruffled.

Greg is usually pretty attuned to what's going on around him, but he didn't seem to notice the looks his two guests were giving each other. If anything, he had a pleased air about him.

"Come on in, Amber."

She hesitated. For a second I thought she was going to turn around and leave, which I couldn't help but think would have been the best thing for everyone. But she didn't. Instead, she took a halting step through the doorway, as if she had turned into a robot and was moving in automation.

"You didn't tell me anyone else was coming," she said to Greg in a flat voice.

"No, I didn't," Greg admitted pleasantly, as though tricking dinner guests was an admirable thing. "I thought it would be a nice surprise."

A nice surprise indeed! Putting two people who can't stand the sight of each other in the same room is rarely a good thing. But then, Greg didn't know how fervently we disliked each other.

Amber took another step forward, still looking slightly dazed. Dr. Taylor had joined them and was extending his hand as Greg introduced them.

"Good to meet you, Amber," he said smiling, "we're glad you could come."

She shook his hand and told him it was nice to meet him too, but there was about as much enthusiasm in her voice as you might expect from a dead fish.

"And you've already met Shelby Belgarden," Greg continued on, oblivious to our mutual aversion toward each other. "She's a very good friend of mine, and I think the two of you will really hit it off."

"*Do* you?" Amber asked in the coldest voice I've ever heard. Then she directed her gaze at me and said "Hello," and her tone was even chillier.

All of a sudden I was the one who wanted to run out of there. Something as cold as her voice settled in my stomach, and in a flash I knew what it was. I hadn't kept the story about how I'd set her up to take my watch quiet for the reasons I'd thought at all. The truth was that I didn't want Greg to find out about it.

I still had no doubt that Amber was the thief, but I knew deep down inside that Greg would never believe it without absolute proof. He'd take the same point of view that Mr. Lower had taken, and worse, he'd think I was wrong for having set the trap in the first place.

My insides churned, and I thought I was going to be sick. What if Amber brought it up? I was sure she'd tell the story in a way that put me in the worst possible light, and I'd have to sit there and face Greg's disapproval. She'd turn her act of theft into a victory of sorts, and I'd be the horrid person who had tried to frame her.

The worst thing was that there was nothing I could do about it. Amber seated herself at the table as Dr. Taylor tossed thin strips of raw chicken into the sizzling wok. I avoided looking at her, but even so I could feel her eyes on me and I knew they held nothing but contempt.

Greg was setting the table and didn't seem to notice how huge the silence in the room had grown. It was the kind of silence that seems to have a life and presence of its own, as if you could actually reach out and touch it. Mercifully, after what seemed an hour but could only have been ten minutes or so, Dr. Taylor announced that dinner was ready and brought two steaming bowls to the table. One held the stir-fry, the other rice.

I spooned small helpings of each onto my plate, wondering how I was going to force myself to eat. I'd managed to get down a few bites when Dr. Taylor made a comment that made my stomach contract even worse.

"Oh, Amber, did you know that our Shelby here is something of a detective?"

"Is she now?" Amber's voice was as polite as all get out, but there was a smirk on her face as she spoke.

"Oh, yes. In fact, she single-handedly figured out who was setting fires in Little River just a few months ago."

"How clever of you, Shelby," Amber looked directly at me, her eyes mocking. "And how is the sleuthing business these days?"

"Actually, it's a bit slow at the moment, but one can always hope for a big crime wave." I spoke in a light, joking manner but knew I was crimson as I answered.

"There's been a rash of thefts at school lately, Dad." Greg injected. "I'm sure that Shelby is right on top of it. I bet she's solving it in her head even as we speak."

"Well, then, I feel safer already," Amber's face was the picture of innocence, but I knew she was toying with me. It put me in mind of the way a cat will let a mouse start to escape after playing with it a little, only to recapture it for the kill.

"By the way, that's a very pretty watch you have on."

"Thanks, Amber," I mumbled. There was *no way* I was going to be able to eat another bite, and I didn't know how I could explain that to Dr. Taylor without seeming rude.

"You came to Little River from somewhere out in Alberta, am I right, Amber?"

I could have hugged Dr. Taylor for changing the subject!

"Yes."

"What part of Alberta?"

"Just a small town northwest of Edmonton." Amber seemed uncomfortable to have been asked about her home.

"Like in the Whitecourt, Valleyview area?"

"You know Alberta quite well," she smiled. "Have you spent time there yourself?"

If Dr. Taylor noticed that she'd avoided answering his question, he didn't show it.

"Spent a few years out west in my youth," he nodded. "Of course, that was a *long* time ago. I'm a bit surprised I can remember back that far."

"You don't seem that old to me. Why, you can't be any older than my —" Amber stopped without finishing her sentence and turned suddenly to Greg. "Could I have a little more rice, please?"

Greg passed the bowl, and I wondered if he'd noticed that there was still rice left on her plate from the first serving she'd taken. It was obvious she'd been about to let something slip and had tried to cover it up with this sudden and unnecessary request.

As the conversation drifted into other neutral topics I found myself relaxing a little and I managed to eat the food I'd taken. Still, it was without any enjoyment. Dr. Taylor is a great cook, but tonight's dinner could have been cardboard for all the pleasure I got from it.

The minute the table had been cleared and the dishes done I told Greg that I wasn't feeling well and was going to have to leave. There was just no way I could take another second of waiting and wondering if Amber was going to bring up the incident at school. She might tell Greg when I wasn't there, but at least I wouldn't have to face him.

"That's a shame, Shelby," Dr. Taylor sympathized. "Let me give you a drive home."

"Thanks, but I think the walk and fresh air will help."

"Amber and I will walk with you," Greg offered.

"That's okay," I mumbled, thinking that the way he'd said "Amber and I" made it sound as if they were a couple. "I wouldn't be very good company right now."

"Well, I'm afraid you're stuck with me," Amber said, joining me at the door. "I have to be at work at seven, so I'm going that way now too."

I could have kicked myself for taking the cowardly way out when I realized she was leaving anyway. I'd just given up the evening with Greg for nothing. And there I was, stuck walking home with the person who'd just ruined everything for me.

We walked without speaking for a good ten minutes, and if it had been up to me it would have stayed like that all the way. But Amber stopped suddenly and turned to face me.

"Are you going out with Greg?" Her question startled me.

"Not exactly," I admitted slowly, wondering why she was asking.

"He's a cool guy." She spoke as if I wasn't there.

I didn't know what to say to that. Was she telling me that she was interested in him? As if she'd read my thoughts, she spoke again.

"If you set me up the other day because you thought I was after Greg, you were wrong."

"*What?*" The idea was preposterous! As if I'd framed her because I was jealous.

"Well, whatever your reason, and I have no idea what it might be, though I've been trying to figure it out, you're on the wrong track. I'm not a thief."

There was something in her face, a kind of angry determination that cut right into me. I looked at her, trying to see past the words, when suddenly her expression crumpled. Amber Chapman, the girl who'd been nothing but cold and aloof since the first time I'd seen her, started to cry!

I reached out and put a hand on her arm.

"I'm sorry," I said, feeling helpless, "I really am." I knew in that moment that I'd been wrong, that Amber was not the one who was stealing things at school.

"It's not even that," she cried softly. And then, between wrenching sobs, Amber spilled out the whole story that she'd been trying so hard to keep inside.

CHAPTER TWELVE

By the time we got to Broderick's, which is just a few blocks from my house, Amber had grown silent again. I couldn't help but wonder if she already regretted telling me about her situation. When I thought about it, it was really strange that she'd confided in me, considering all the unpleasantness that had occurred between us. Maybe she figured that if I was a friend of Greg's there must be something good about me.

"Amber," I ventured just before we would be parting company, "I want you to know that I'll respect your privacy. You can trust me."

I was hoping to alleviate any worry she had that I might blab her story all over the place. The way she looked relieved at my words, I knew I'd been right. "Thanks. I wasn't going to tell anyone," she said quietly, "but it was building up and I really needed to talk about it."

"I'm glad you did."

"And to *you*!" she smiled wryly. "I'd never have guessed that was going to happen."

"Me neither." I was glad now that I'd left Greg's place early. Who knows if things would ever have changed between us if I hadn't? "I'm really sorry about, well, everything."

"Thanks. Well, I'd better get to work."

"Amber, before you go, there's something I want to say. Please don't take it the wrong way, but I think you're taking the wrong approach to living here. If you could just relax a bit and get to know people, make some friends, I'm sure things would be easier for you."

"I know you're right, and I'll try, but it's so hard to trust anyone after what happened."

I watched her walk away, thinking how small her shoulders were to be carrying such a heavy load. When she'd disappeared inside the gas station I turned and continued home.

Mom was there, and she was surprised to see me back so early.

"I thought you had plans with Greg this evening. Is everything okay?"

"Yeah, there's no problem or anything. I just wasn't feeling good."

She looked alarmed right away, and I knew what she was about to say as she hurried toward me. Mom is pretty predictable at times.

"Let me feel your forehead."

I rolled my eyes, the way I always do when Mom makes a big fuss for no reason. Sometimes it seems that she's hovering over me, just waiting for a chance to do motherly stuff like that.

"Well, you're not running a temperature. Does anything hurt?"

"No, Mom. I think I'm just overtired and out of sorts. I'll be fine."

"You're sure you don't have a headache or tummy ache or anything?"

"I'm sure." I was already planning my escape to avoid any more of her quizzing. Then I remembered what Amber had just told me. It really hit me just what it means to have a mother who cares enough to fuss.

"Thanks though, Mom." I gave her a quick hug. "I'm going to lay down for a bit, but I'll let you know if I need you."

She looked pleased and a little surprised. Usually I'm pretty resistant to her fretting and worrying, so I guess my appreciation was kind of unexpected. Thinking about that on the way to my bedroom I realized that I don't often show a lot of gratitude for the way my parents take care of me. Of course, they're old and all, and they can get on my nerves at times with their old folks' ways and ideas, but maybe that's not so bad after all.

There are certainly worse things! I lay on my bed and thought about Amber's situation, and it nearly made me cry. It's no wonder that she came to Little River determined to keep to herself. I'd probably do the same thing if something like that had ever happened to me.

Amber grew up in Alberta and had lived with her parents until she was ten. Then her folks got a divorce, which happens to lots of kids. But what happened after that is really sad.

At first she and her older brother lived with their mom, and when it was just the three of them everything seemed to be okay. She was used to not having her dad around anyway, because of his work.

Amber's father works for a big company that has offices all over the world, and he's always being sent to live in other countries. She only sees him a couple of times a year, when he's in Canada on leaves from his job. I'd hate that, but I guess if that's what a person is used to it would seem normal.

Anyway, there were no big problems until a couple of years ago, when everything changed. Amber's mom started dating another man, and at first it seemed that he was a pretty good guy. He'd take them all to the movies or out to dinner, and he was friendly and nice to her and her brother.

"My mom was just gone on him," Amber had told me. "She started changing when Pete came into our lives. At the start it was little things, like the way she wore her hair. It used to be long and full, but Pete likes women with short hair, so she got it cut. It didn't stop with that, though, because they got married and before I knew it we were doing everything the way Pete wanted it. It was 'Pete doesn't like your music, so wear earphones when you're listening to your CDs.' Or 'Pete thinks five minutes is long enough to talk on the phone at one time.' And it just went on and on, until our whole house was like Pete's prison."

I'd listened as she continued, wondering what it would be like to have a stranger come into your house and start telling you what to do about every little thing.

"It went on and on, like some nightmare that just kept getting worse, except you didn't wake up from it. Pete's favourite expression was 'it's not suitable.' My friends couldn't come over to the house anymore because Pete didn't think they were suitable. I told Mom it wasn't fair, they were my friends, and she just took his side and said he was doing it for my own good. My own good! Nothing was for my good, it was all for Pete. What he wanted was the way it was going to be.

"Pete was the *man* of the house, he was in *control*. It wasn't suitable for me to wear makeup. It wasn't suitable for me to put posters up in my room. My clothes weren't suitable for a young lady; they embarrassed him. I've been dressing like this since I was about twelve. I like coming up with my own look, something that's unique. I'm going to be a fashion designer when I finish college, though Pete probably wouldn't think that was suitable either. There were constant wars in the house, and Mom would never open her mouth to stand up for me. She just agreed with everything he said. I think she was terrified he'd leave her if she didn't.

"Then Pete decided that he and Mom needed more time for themselves. He makes this big announcement at the table one night, and Mom actually sat there and smiled as if it was a wonderful idea. He tells me that I have to give them more privacy and that from now on I'm not to disturb them three evenings during the school week or anytime on Saturday. So I ask him how I'm supposed to give them all this privacy and he says I can just stay in my room!

"Well, I was furious and told him there was *no way* I was going to be sent to my room like a little kid, that it was my house too and I had rights. And he says I'm spoiled rotten and I have no consideration for anyone else and if I don't like it I can get out."

She'd been crying hard by this point in her story and had to stop and get herself pulled together before she could go on.

"Just like that — if I don't like it I can leave. My way or the highway, he says. So I turned to Mom and asked her if she was going to let him talk to me like that, but she had her head down and wouldn't look at me. Then after a few minutes she says that since I'm always causing trouble with Pete and won't listen to him, maybe it would be better for everyone if I lived somewhere else. Better for everyone all right. It sure didn't sound like it would be better for me.

"I couldn't believe what I'd just heard! My *mother*, telling me *I* was the one creating all the problems. The worst part was that she seemed perfectly willing to throw me out of my own house just to make him happy."

It was impossible for me to imagine what it would be like to have my mom choose some man over me.

"Well, the three of us had the biggest fight ever, and at the end of it they tell me I'm going to be sent here. Just think of it! They'd already arranged the whole thing and were just waiting for some big blow-up so they'd have an excuse."

"That's horrible, Amber," was all I could think to say.

"I hope they're happy now, with all that privacy and doing everything that Pete thinks is suitable." There was bitterness in her voice, and I couldn't blame her a bit. "When I was leaving Mom started crying and saying she was sorry it had to be that way. I didn't even bother pointing out that it didn't *have* to be that way at all, there had been a choice and she'd made it. I just walked away from her and got on the plane and never looked back."

"Does your mom phone or write or anything?"

"She called a couple of times, but I wouldn't talk to her. The Brodericks were pretty understanding about that, too, and didn't try to persuade me to take her calls. They're nice people, but even though they're relatives and all I barely know them. I only met them a couple of times before all this happened. She hasn't written, but if she did I'd just send the letters back."

"What about your dad?"

"He phones and sends me things, and he's coming to see me before the end of the school year, but it will only be for a couple of weeks. I guess his job is more important to him than me."

It was no wonder that Amber had come to Little River with the attitude she had. I don't think I'd want to trust anyone or get close to people if something like that had happened to me.

And now she had to deal with the kids at school thinking she was a thief on top of everything else. I felt so ashamed when I thought of what I'd done and how I'd been so willing to think the worst of her.

Now the most important thing I could do was to help clear her name. I was determined to do just that.

CHAPTER THIRTEEN

Greg was working on Saturday, which was probably just as well since when I got up that morning there was a zit growing right in the middle of my nose. It was bright red and sore to touch, like some angry volcano that couldn't quite decide to erupt. I didn't care that it hurt, but I sure cared that it was there.

When I went down to breakfast Mom and Dad were in the kitchen talking about what colour to paint the living room. Mom was discussing it as if Dad actually had a vote, which was pretty silly. Dad can't even put together a pair of pants and shirt without asking if the colours match. I've seen him looking really perplexed when Mom tries to explain that something clashes. It amazes me that he can't just see it himself. I have two theories on the subject. I think that most men are either missing the part of the brain that understands colour combinations, or they just don't care.

Betts once broke up with a guy because it seemed every time they went somewhere he had the same shirt on.

"I just couldn't take it anymore," she'd told me. "He wore it everywhere we went. Can you imagine? Every time we went out! I was starting to fantasize about ways to ruin it. Like spilling mustard on it or something."

"Why didn't you just tell him? He probably didn't even notice. You know how guys are — they couldn't tell you what they wore yesterday! Or maybe it was his favourite shirt and he wanted to look good for you."

"Yeah, well he can just look good for someone else."

And that was that. I felt kind of sorry for him because he really liked Betts a lot and he went around school looking sad for weeks after she ditched him. I bet he'd never have guessed that he'd been dumped because of a shirt!

I got thinking about that and decided to test Dad on the subject.

"Dad, what did you wear last weekend when you and Mom went to visit the Parkers?"

"What did I wear? Now that's a strange question."

"I'm just curious to see if you remember. It was only a week ago."

"Checking for signs of early Alzheimer's are you?"

"No, I just have this theory."

"Well, let's see. I think it might have been, uh, maybe it was, you know I'm just not sure."

"You're not *sure*? You mean you have no idea whatsoever."

"No, I guess I don't." He laughed, admitting this.

"What about you, Mom?"

"I wore my black skirt and ecru blouse. Your father had on his pale blue shirt and dark gray pants."

She didn't even have to think about it; she just knew. Dad shrugged helplessly and glanced back and forth between us, as if we were ganging up on him and his only chance to escape ridicule was to elicit our sympathy.

"It's okay, Dad," I patted his arm. "You can't help it. That's just the way male brains work."

"Well, we men have other things, *important* things, on our minds," he insisted.

"Like who's the best pound-for-pound boxer in the world at the moment?" I asked cheekily.

"Heck, nothing to wonder about there. It's Roy Jones Junior, no matter what some of these upstart sports commentators may think. Jones has dominated every weight division he's gone through. Why, his speed, power, and agility make him one of the best boxers of all time, right up there with Ali and Robinson...!"

Dad trailed off sheepishly while Mom gave me a look that said "see what you've started?" When Dad gets talking about boxing he can go on for any length of time!

"That's much more important than clothes," I said deadpan.

"Shelby, I almost forgot to tell you that you had a letter yesterday." Mom spoke up quickly. I could see she was glad to have a chance to change the subject as she passed me an envelope. Her words had the desired effect of sending me off to another room where I wouldn't be getting Dad all wound up over something she didn't want to listen to.

The letter was from my friend Jane, who'd moved away from Little River a month ago. I tore it open, eager for news of how she was doing, and was happy to read that they were settled and that she liked her new school.

> I miss my friends, but things aren't so bad. Mom and I are spending a lot of time talking and sorting out what happened. She blames herself for a lot of it, and I guess I blame her too, in a way. But things are getting better, and I think we're going to be all right.
>
> I have a new probation officer here, a Ms. Gladstone, who's really nice and understanding. She made arrangements for me to get into a survivors group, and I went for the

*first time last week. It was kind of scary at
first, but it's a good group and I think I'm
going to make some friends there.*

I read Jane's letter twice, glad to know she was
doing all right. She'd been through a lot and had
been in some trouble, but she seemed to be finding
her way okay now. After writing a long, newsy letter
back, I decided to take it to a mailbox and stop at the
drugstore to get some zit cream on my way home. If
I didn't get rid of the hideous blight on my nose
before Monday, I'd have to wear a bag over my head
for school.

I'd dropped the letter in the mail slot, made my
purchase, and was on the way home when I saw someone sitting hunched over and shaking on a bench in the
town square. There was something familiar about the
person, and I could see it was a teenage boy, so I walked
over that way, ignoring the risk of having my erupting
nose seen.

As I got close I saw that it was Tony Carter and
wished I hadn't been so nosy. I'd have kept on right by
without talking but he glanced up and saw me.

"Hi, Tony," I mumbled half-heartedly. I noticed
then that his face was unusually pale, and it occurred
to me that maybe he was sick and needed help. "Are
you okay?"

"Yeah, I'm all right." His tone belied the words but there was no point in pressing the matter. A large duffel bag sat beside him on the ground. I noticed that it had a bus tag on it and remembered his mom telling me he spent most weekends at the college with his brother.

"Not in Veander this weekend?" I felt stupid as soon as asked this. It was the dumb kind of question that I hate other people asking. Obviously, if he was sitting here on a bench, he wasn't in Veander!

"I was, but I got bored and came home early." His eyes narrowed as he looked at me, and I realized he must be wondering how I knew he usually spent his weekends there. He was probably thinking I liked him or something, and was keeping tabs on him. I blushed, wanting away from there as quickly as possible.

"That's too bad." I figured the rest of my face had probably grown red enough to match the zit on my nose. "Well, see you around."

He mumbled something that I couldn't quite hear as I hurried away. Of all the bad luck! Well, I guess it wasn't just bad luck. I had to accept the fact that my nosiness had a lot to do with what had just happened. And speaking without thinking! It reminded me of a poster I'd seen once that had a list of rules about talking. One of them said something like "Do not engage mouth while brain is in neutral." Well, that's exactly what I'd just done.

Now Tony probably thought I had some big crush on him and was keeping track of everything he did. The worst part was that he might start telling other people. It would certainly get back to Greg if he did. Someone would get great enjoyment out of telling him. That's just the way people are.

It was just a little before two o'clock when I got home, and I managed to worry about the whole thing for the rest of the afternoon.

CHAPTER FOURTEEN

Sunday afternoon found me still fretting a little over the incident with Tony, but I'd managed to remind myself of something Dad told me a long time ago. He said that if you see ten problems coming down the road toward you, nine of them are sure to run into the ditch before they ever reach you. I was hoping that this was one of the nine.

Greg had called just before lunch and asked if I had any plans later. I'd agreed to meet him at the Scream Machine at two o'clock. The zit on my nose was still pretty angry looking, but I figured I could hide it fairly well with a bit of makeup. I doctored it up the best I could, slipped on a teal sweater and black jeans, and went off to see him.

He was already there when I arrived, even though I was ten minutes early. That made me feel good because it meant he was as anxious to see me as I was to see him.

"Hey!" he smiled and stood as I walked toward the booth where he was sitting.

"Hey, yourself." I slid into the empty side and met his smile with one of my own.

"Are you hungry?"

"Naw, I just had lunch a while ago."

"So did I, but we men can always go for a little snack."

"Well, snack away. I'll just have a bottle of water."

Greg's "snack" turned out to be a double cheeseburger platter and a chocolate shake. When he'd finished those he picked up the menu, which is a single, plastic-coated page with burgers and stuff on one side and beverages and desserts on the other. I saw that he was studying the dessert side with some interest.

"Their coconut cream pie is good," he commented. "But then, the cheesecake looks pretty tempting too."

"Some snack," I teased.

"I have to eat well to maintain these massive muscles," he defended himself.

"Guys are disgusting," I complained. "You can just stuff your faces any time you want and never gain an ounce. Girls can't get away with that. We gain weight just looking at food! It's not fair."

"Well, try not to let it make you bitter," he snickered. Then he ordered the pie *and* the cheesecake!

They both looked delicious, and when he offered me some, I gave in, pointed to the pie, and giggled as he scooped up a bite and fed it to me. It was scrumptious. Then he passed me one of the forks and we ended up sharing both desserts. We fed each other and pretended we didn't notice the waitress's amused glances.

"Oh, no!" he exclaimed just as we'd finished the last crumbs of the cheesecake. He was looking at me in horror.

"What? Do I have whipped cream on my face or something?"

"No," he shielded his eyes. "I'm afraid it's much worse than that."

"It's my zit, isn't it?" The makeup had probably come off when I wiped my face. I put my hand up to cover it instinctively.

"Is that a zit? I thought you were growing a second nose."

"Hey!" I tossed a crumpled napkin at him.

"Anyway, it's not the zit."

"Well then, what is it?"

He leaned forward, glanced around quickly as if to make sure no one was listening, and whispered, "I think you've gained a tenth of an ounce from eating that dessert."

"Oh, stop it!" I laughed.

"No, seriously, you're ballooning out even as we speak. In fact, we'd better hurry up and leave while you can still squeeze through the doorway."

"You, sir, are a cur," I told him, using a line I'd seen in a movie once. "Besides, you wouldn't find it so funny if your ..." I paused, realizing I'd been about to say "girlfriend," which was a bit presumptuous since he'd never actually asked me out. "I mean, it would be a different story if I really was fat."

"How's that?"

"Well, you wouldn't be, uh ..." I trailed off again.

"Interested in you?" he prompted. "I *am* interested in you, you know. It's all right to say it."

"Okay then," I felt giddy all of a sudden. "You wouldn't be interested in me if I was overweight."

"And why not?"

"Because guys are like that."

"Some guys are," he admitted, "but that just means *they* have a problem. You'd have to be pretty shallow to judge someone on that basis. The things that count are inside a person, not outside. Anyone who doesn't know that isn't worth bothering with anyway."

I thought about Annie Berkley and Todd Saunders, a couple who seemed to be a mismatch at first. They'd started going out last December, and everyone had been a bit surprised. Todd is something of a jock and Annie is kind of chubby. But now that they'd been dating for a while, it was obvious that they were really happy with each other. You could see that Todd was crazy about Annie, the way he looked at her with such pride and affection.

Greg got up to pay our bill, and I went to the girls' room to check my nose. It looked bad, but I hadn't thought to bring any foundation with me so there wasn't much I could do about it. I fixed my hair a bit and went back out to find Greg waiting by the door.

"Ready to go?"

"Sure. Where are we going?"

"You're always so nosy!" He reached over and took my hand. "Though I suppose that's why you're such a famous and successful detective."

"Yeah, I'm famous all right. That's why we're thronged with people begging for my autograph." Greg knew perfectly well that I'd only solved one mystery and that I'd actually almost bungled it.

"No doubt your clever disguise of an extra nose is the only thing saving you from the autograph seekers."

I gave him a playful punch on the arm. He suggested I get my violent nature under control. We walked along laughing and talking nonsense until we reached a wooded road leading out of town.

"This way," he instructed, leading me along a path that wound through the woods and down to the river. The deciduous trees were budding with green bursts of spring growth and the whole place smelled gloriously of new life.

There's a certain kind of stillness in the forest that makes you feel you should be quiet, and as our conversation faded I became aware of the sounds of the woods. What first seemed an almost silent place was actually a symphony of birdcalls blended with rustling trees and other sounds. I felt almost like an intruder in another world.

We emerged at the river when we'd reached the path's end and Greg lead me along the shore until we got to a spot where the bank was impassible. After a quick detour back through the woods we came out at the river once again. It was a spot I'd never been to before.

"Here we are." He pointed to a large rock formation that jutted out over the water. "I found this place one day last fall. Isn't it great?"

"It's awesome!"

He helped me out onto the largest of the rocks, and I was delighted to find that there was a slight dip in the end of it. It looked as though it was indented purposely for two people to sit there. I slid into the spot and let my legs hang over the edge, feeling the sharp coolness of the breeze off the water. Greg slipped in beside me, and a thrill went all through me as his arm reached around my back. His hand settled on my shoulder, and I automatically reached mine up to hold his.

I'm not sure how long we sat there in silence. It was the kind of thing that you just don't want to end. The beauty of nature was all around, and it caused a kind of sensory overload with the sights and sounds and smells. I drifted into a state of contentment that was so deep it felt as though I was falling asleep.

In my drowsiness my head slid over to rest on Greg's shoulder. Then his free hand reached up and touched the side of my face.

"Shelby," his voice was barely a whisper. "This is where I wanted to bring you that Saturday when we had to cancel our plans."

"It's the most perfect place I've ever been," I murmured.

"It is, isn't it? I thought it would be just the right spot to ask you if you'd go out with me."

My heart was pounding so hard I couldn't speak. All the sleepiness had fled off, chased away by overwhelming happiness.

"Well? Will you?"

All I could do was nod. And then he was leaning over and kissing me.

CHAPTER FIFTEEN

Being kissed was even better than I'd imagined. It made me all weak and tingly, as if everything inside had turned into some kid of warm, fuzzy jelly. Mostly, though, it filled me with the most amazingly happy feeling. It was a good thing that we stayed there on the rock for a while before heading back home because I don't think my legs would have worked right then.

When we did leave, Greg stopped along the riverbank and leaned down to pick up a couple of stones. They were round and smooth, and he rubbed them in his hand to get off the bits of sand that clung to them. Then he passed one to me.

"We'll each keep one of these to remember today by," he said, kissing my forehead.

I knew I'd never forget one single moment of the day, but I took the stone gladly and slipped it into my pocket. My fingers curled around it as we walked along the path and back out to the road.

I hadn't realized how late it was getting. By the time I got home, Mom and Dad were almost finished eating dinner.

"Come right on in, Greg," Dad called out when he saw us in the doorway. "Darlene and I were just going to send out a search party for Shelby, but since you've brought her back safe and sound after all I guess we could give you a bite to eat."

"Yes, Greg, come and join us," Mom agreed, jumping up to fetch an extra plate.

"I'd like to, I really would," Greg's voice was apologetic. "But I've been out of the house most of the weekend, what with work and all. I think I should get home and spend some time with Dad."

Mom nodded understandingly. I guess that being a widower Dr. Taylor is probably lonely and finds the time long when Greg isn't home much.

"Well, another time soon then," Dad waved his fork. "You're always welcome here."

I'd have thought that the excitement of the afternoon would have made it nearly impossible to eat but quite the opposite was true. Mom had made her special sweet and sour meatballs and rice, and the smell made me realize just how hungry I was. I scooped a big helping onto my plate and was busy devouring it when I noticed how still and quiet the room had gotten. Looking up, I saw Mom and Dad watching me.

"Well?" Mom asked with this huge smile on her face.

"Well, what?"

"How was your afternoon?"

"Fine." I should have known she'd start fishing for information!

"Anything exciting happen?"

"Like what?"

"Like your first kiss perhaps?"

"Mom! Why do you have to be so nosy?" I popped another meatball into my mouth.

"She doesn't *have* to be nosy," Dad said with a grin. "She just likes to."

"I'm not *nosy*," Mom insisted. "I'm just *interested* in my child. Is that so wrong?"

I was about to point out that some things are private, but before I got a chance to swallow my food, Dad spoke up again.

"Anyway, dear, I think you should know that your mother and I approve of Greg. He's a nice boy, just the kind of young fellow that we'd have picked out for you ourselves. Isn't that right, Darlene?"

Mom nodded, but I could tell she hadn't been completely distracted from wanting to dig information out of me.

I suppose they meant this to be reassuring. Of all the crazy ideas! What teenage girl wants to date someone that her *parents* would have picked out for her? If I didn't like Greg so much, it would have been enough to make me ditch him.

"He's a lovely boy," Mom piped up. "Now you be sure to invite your young man over for dinner sometime soon."

"A lovely boy!" "Your young man." It never ceases to amaze me that my folks can say things in such dumb ways — and without even realizing it.

"Speaking of dinner," I snapped, "it sure would be nice to be able to eat mine in peace."

"Well, Randall, it looks as though we're not good enough to be informed of the happenings in our daughter's life."

"Now, sweetheart, I'm sure Shelby's just tired and hungry." Dad always sticks up for me. Mom wasn't mollified, though. She picked up the dishes they'd finished with and went to the sink with her face all piled up in a pout.

"We do everything for that child. Everything. And then when I ask a simple question she shuts me out as if I'm nothing but a bother to her. I guess that's the thanks we get for trying to be good parents."

"I guess so," I muttered under my breath.

"What was that?"

"Nothing."

"It wasn't *nothing*. Now what did you say?"

"I said I guess so."

Mom's eyes had gone into a squint, and I could see she was trying to remember what she'd said first, so that she could find fault with me saying "I guess so." She gave up after a minute and turned back to the sink with a shrug.

Dad shifted in his chair, and I felt sorry for him. He's always been the family peacemaker, and he hates it when there's any tension in the house. Thank goodness we don't have very many arguments. I don't think he could take it.

"Now girls," he said with a heavy sigh, "let's not spoil the evening. Why don't we all take a drive, maybe pick up a movie and some treats?"

"Okay," I said quickly, sure that Mom wouldn't agree with the suggestion. But she surprised me and told Dad that she'd have to finish the dishes first and then we could go.

I finished eating, took my plate to the sink, picked up the drying towel, and started helping.

"The meatballs were great, Mom. Thanks."

She nodded stiffly without answering, and I saw that her face was all set and tight, as if she was on the verge of crying and holding herself from it.

It made me feel so bad. I suppose I could have been a bit nicer, even if she was prying. I guess if I was grown up and had a teenage daughter I'd probably want to know about special things that happened to her too.

"You were right about the smacking noise," I said, concentrating on drying a plate. In my peripheral vision I could see her take a quick glance at me. A flicker of a smile crossed her lips but she pushed it down. It seemed she wanted to sulk a bit longer, which is what she usually does when something has upset her. I knew she was probably dying to know if Greg had asked me out, but when she's in that kind of mood she's too stubborn to ask questions.

I guess I inherited a bit of her stubbornness because I didn't say any more on the subject, even though I suddenly wanted to tell her all about it. We finished cleaning up the dishes and kitchen and then got our jackets and told Dad we were ready to go.

"Excellent!" he boomed with forced cheer. He talked non-stop in the same tone as we drove toward Nick's Flicks, one of our local movie stores.

We were about halfway there when we heard a siren. Dad had to pull to the side of the road to let the police car pass. I cranked my neck to see the officers in the front seat of the car, and they looked grim and excited all at once.

We don't have much crime in Little River, so the sound of a siren caught everyone's attention. Faces started appearing in windows right away. Some folks came right out of their houses, and a few people even got in their cars and started off in the direction the police had gone.

I could tell that Dad was itching to see what was going on too, but he wouldn't dare follow the police. Mom would have wigged out and started a big lecture on minding your own business and not getting in the officers' way.

It turned out that we got to see a bit of what was happening anyway because the action was right on our route. The police cruiser had come to a stop at Broderick's Gas Bar and the officers were already inside. I got a glimpse of a pale face turned toward the men in uniforms.

I didn't know it then, but things were about to get a lot worse for Amber Chapman.

CHAPTER SIXTEEN

Curiosity was getting the best of me after seeing the police cars at Broderick's. I tried to push it aside and concentrate on picking out a movie but in the end I just went along with one Dad suggested. It didn't matter anyway, since I couldn't keep my mind on it once we were back home and it was playing.

When the phone rang halfway through the movie I jumped up to get it.

"Never mind stopping the show," I told Dad as I saw him reach for the remote control, "I'll just catch up when I get back." The truth was I had only a vague idea of the story line anyway. I grabbed the phone on the third ring, hoping it might be Betts calling to tell me the latest local news. Instead, it was Greg's voice that I heard after I'd said "Hello."

"I'm at work," he told me quickly. "The gas bar was

held up a little while ago and the police have taken Amber to the station to get a statement from her. Mr. Broderick wanted to go down there too, so he asked me to come in."

"Held up? You mean it was robbed?" I was shocked. We've had a few break and enters in Little River, but this was the first time I'd ever heard of a business being robbed. "What happened?"

"Amber was working tonight when someone came in wearing a mask. He held a gun to her and demanded all the cash. I don't know much more than that about it."

"A gun!" I could hardly believe it. "That's horrible. She must have been scared out of her mind."

"Probably. She was already gone when I got here so I haven't talked to her. Mr. Broderick was anxious to get to the station and just gave me a quick rundown of what had happened."

"Poor Mr. Broderick," I thought aloud. "He's such a nice old guy. Who would do something like that to him?"

"I don't think that thieves are generally all that interested in whether the person they rob is nice or not."

"I suppose not. Still, Mr. Broderick is well loved in this town. Maybe it was someone passing through, someone who didn't know him."

"Could be. But he said the person was on foot. That makes it sound like a local did it."

"Or the getaway car was parked out of sight so the license plate number couldn't be taken."

"That's possible. But there are ways to hide a license plate." Greg seemed distracted all of a sudden. "And walking really increases the chance of being caught before you get away. Look, I've got to go now. There's a customer coming in."

We said goodbye and I went to fill Mom and Dad in on the latest news. They were as surprised as I'd been to learn that the police we'd seen earlier had been responding to a robbery. Mom laid aside her counted cross-stitch work and told Dad she was going to see Mrs. Broderick.

"I don't think she should be alone right now," she explained. "She's probably feeling a bit scared and unsettled by this whole thing. I'll go over and stay with her until her husband gets back from the police station."

Mom is like that. Most people who might think of going over to the Broderick's house at a time like that would only be doing it to see what they could find out. Not Mom. She was genuinely worried about the older woman and wanted to make sure she was okay.

Shortly after that there was a knock at the door and I found Betts standing there, her eyes all lit up with excitement.

"Did you hear?" she gasped rushing into the kitchen. "Broderick's gas station was robbed a while ago."

She was clearly disappointed when I told her that I already knew about the robbery. Betts likes to be the first one to know about things. I guess it makes her feel important to tell news to someone who hasn't heard it yet. I'm not sure why that is, but it explains why it's so hard for most folks to keep a secret. Mom always says that if you can't keep a secret yourself, it shouldn't surprise you if the person you told it to can't keep it either.

I learned the truth in that a few years ago. I learned it the hard way, too.

One of our teachers at school had given us an assignment to teach us about being entrepreneurs. We had to come up with our own moneymaking projects, carry them out, and then write up a financial report.

Everyone had different ideas of what to do. Some kids organized car washes and yard sales and stuff like that. Others sold tickets on different things. Mine was a ticket draw too, but a bit different from the ones where you just put all the slips of paper in a bag and haul one out.

What I did was fill a big old jar that Mom found for me with all sorts of candies. It took a lot to fill it, and I had to count them, which took forever because I kept losing track and had to start over. Anyway, when I was done, I sold tickets where people guessed how many candies there were in the jar. The winner would be the person who came closest to the actual number.

Well, Betts wasn't going to buy a guess, because we figured it would look suspicious if she happened to win, seeing as she's my best friend and all. And because of that, she kept pestering me to tell her how many candies the jar held.

I finally gave in and told her, then swore her not to tell a soul. The very next day, when I had my display set up outside the cafeteria, Molly, who was a friend of ours, came along and bought a ticket. Her guess was the exact number in the jar.

I was suspicious right away, because I knew she'd been over to Betts's house the night before. I cornered Betts and after a bit of badgering she admitted that she'd told Molly.

When I asked her why she did it, she just said that Molly had insisted that she wasn't interested in buying a ticket, so it had seemed safe to tell her.

As cross as I was with Betts, I had to admit that none of it would have happened if I hadn't told her in the first place. The whole thing was a big mess then, because I couldn't give it to Molly even though she had the right number. I talked it over with Dad and he suggested I toss in a few more candies so that her answer wouldn't be right. That seemed almost like cheating, but I reminded myself she'd cheated too. I put in some more jellybeans, and when the tickets were all sold there was another answer closer to the new total.

You'd think that a person who'd done what Molly did wouldn't have anything to say about it, but she was furious. She came to my locker after school and demanded to know why she hadn't won. I asked her what made her so sure her guess was right, and after stammering and stuttering she walked away. That was pretty much the end of our friendship.

Now when I'm tempted to tell anyone something I don't want spread around, I remind myself of the candy jar and I keep it to myself.

Of course, that's not the same thing as news like the holdup at Broderick's. A story like that will fly around with lightning speed.

It was the turn the story took that was the real surprise.

CHAPTER SEVENTEEN

I got to school at the usual time on Monday morning and went to my locker to get the books I needed for morning classes. There was a buzz of talk all around me, but I was looking for my math textbook and not paying any particular mind to what was being said.

Kelly MacDonald's locker is next to mine, and she was the one who made sure I got the news, leaning her head close as if she was sharing a big secret. The truth was there was nothing secret about the story that was rushing from person to person that morning.

"Did you hear about Amber Chapman?"

"You mean the robbery? Yeah, I heard it."

"Well, I can tell you, I'm not a bit surprised," she whispered breathlessly. "Now maybe they'll get her for all the missing stuff at school too."

My confusion over what she'd said must have shown on my face, because she continued without prompting.

"You *do* know that the police are going to charge Amber with the robbery, don't you?"

"What?" I was stunned. "The robbery at Broderick's?"

"That's right." Kelly looked smug. "They're searching the area around the gas station right now, to see where she hid the money. As soon as they find it, she's toast."

"At least that will be the end of her snooty ways at school," Brianne Daniels chimed in from behind Kelly. "I can't even stand the sight of her, going around as if she's too good for everyone else, when she's nothing but a thief."

I extracted myself from the conversation with a weak comment that I had to find Betts before class. Walking away I felt a huge knot growing in my stomach. Could I have been wrong about Amber? My thoughts raced, going back and forth from my earlier suspicions to the certainty I'd felt in her innocence after the night we'd talked.

As I made my way along the corridor I found myself looking for her. If I got a chance to talk to her some of the new doubts might settle themselves. But she was nowhere in sight, and before long I heard someone remark that she wasn't in school that day.

Who could blame her? If I was being accused of something like that, I wouldn't be keen on facing everyone either. Then another thought occurred to me. Maybe she was absent because she'd already been arrested!

Up ahead I saw Greg standing with a group of guys. He looked grim, and I figured he was hearing the same story Kelly had just told me. Hurrying toward him, I felt a rush of relief. I could count on Greg to take a fair view on the whole thing. He'd never accept anyone's opinion without all the facts.

He looked up and saw me as I neared him. He stepped away from the group and faced me with a forced smile.

"This is bad," I blurted as soon as I'd reached his side. "It's really bad."

"It's ridiculous," he said drawing me to a quiet spot in the hallway where we could talk privately. "And I'm afraid that the rumours are true."

"What do you mean?"

"The police think Amber is guilty. They kept her at the station for hours last night. Mr. Broderick told me about it when he came by at closing time. They told her right out that they think she did it and she might as well confess."

"But why?"

"From what I can figure out their whole theory seems to be that since she's new in town and there's never been a robbery like this before, she must be guilty."

"That's hardly proof."

"It doesn't sound much like they're that interested in proof. They've got this idea and they're planning to make it stick."

"I heard that they're searching the area around the gas station this morning, looking for the money."

"That's true too. They cordoned the whole block off last night and had officers stationed to watch that no one came around."

"So if they don't find anything, they'll have to admit they were wrong about Amber?"

"Not necessarily. She was alone there from five o'clock until almost seven when the robbery occurred. If they stay with this theory, they'll just figure she had time to take the money and hide it somewhere further away before she phoned and reported that the place had been robbed."

"But what about customers? There must have been people who can confirm she was there the whole time."

"That's the worst part," Greg sighed heavily. "Apparently some guy pulled in for gas about ten or fifteen minutes before she called the police. He says the place was empty, so he went down the road to another station."

That sounded bad. Doubts nagged at me again and I struggled to push them aside. "Then where was she?" I asked.

"She swears she never left the station and that she must have been in the bathroom at the time. Of course, the police see it differently. They view it as proof that she was off somewhere hiding the money."

"What does old man Broderick think? I mean, does he think she might be guilty?"

"No way. He told me that he and his wife will stand behind her one hundred percent."

"Do you think the police will really charge her?"

"I don't know, but it doesn't look good. One thing is sure, she's really going to need her friends right now."

I knew he was right, but I also got a scared feeling at the idea. The Brodericks could stand behind Amber and everyone would accept that because they're her relatives. But anyone at school who showed her any kind of support was in for a rough time of it. She was, at that moment, the most unpopular person at Little River High. Heck, she'd been unpopular *before* this happened! Taking her side was going to be hard, and I didn't know if I had enough courage to do it.

The expression on my face must have told Greg what I was thinking, because he took my hand and spoke gently.

"It's never easy to go against the crowd, but sometimes a person has no choice."

"Well, wouldn't it be enough just to stay neutral, not take sides at all?" Even as I asked the question, I knew what Greg would see as the right answer.

"You have to decide that for yourself." In spite of his gentle tone I felt sure he was disappointed in me.

"Look, Greg, I hardly even know Amber." I said defensively. "It's not like she's my best friend. I don't owe her anything."

"It's not a question of what you owe Amber," he smiled wryly, "it's what you owe yourself. You've got to live with whatever you choose to do now."

That hit me hard, and I suddenly felt like crying. But the bell rang then and we had to hurry off to our classes.

It stayed with me all day, and at lunchtime I felt guilty listening to Betts talk about the whole thing. She, like almost everyone else, was ready to find Amber guilty.

I stayed silent, even though I could feel Greg's eyes on me. I knew he was watching to see what I'd do, but it just wasn't in me to speak up for Amber.

Besides, maybe the police were right. How was I to know what was true?

The one truth that was settling on me quickly was that I wasn't brave enough to stick my neck out for a girl I barely knew.

CHAPTER EIGHTEEN

Amber wasn't at school on Tuesday either, and there was talk that she'd been arrested. It turned out that wasn't true, as I learned from Greg. He'd worked the night before and old man Broderick had filled him in on what was new.

Apparently the police's search for the missing money had turned up nothing. They'd gone through every possible hiding place in a two-block radius from the gas station and had even checked the Brodericks' house from top to bottom, on the chance that Amber might have gotten to the money before they did. I thought that was a stupid idea. If she was guilty, the last place she'd stash the cash would be the house she was living in.

They'd also picked her up and questioned her again, at which point the Brodericks insisted on getting a lawyer. Greg told me that the lawyer had told the police she wouldn't be answering any more questions, and since she wasn't being charged they had to release her. Still, it was clear they were getting more and more determined to prove that she was responsible for the theft.

A statement had been issued asking for anyone who might know anything about the crime to come forward. And a reward of five hundred dollars was offered if the information led to a conviction.

I guess giving a reward can help the police solve a crime, but it also struck me it could lead to its own problems too. After all, there was nothing to prevent a person from inventing a story just to get the reward. It made me nervous to think about the possibility that Amber could be convicted on false testimony.

And that's what almost happened. Of all the people who might do such a thing, I would never have guessed Mrs. Carter would be the one, but that's exactly who it was. Even though I don't much like her, mainly because of the way she traps you with longwinded and boring conversations, I wouldn't have thought her capable of such an underhanded thing.

Still, facts are facts. Greg heard about it from old man Broderick, who had learned she'd gone to the police and given them a statement. She told them that she'd been driving along the street near the gas station just before the robbery and had seen Amber sneaking through someone's backyard with a bag under her arm.

It seems that the police were getting ready to swear out a warrant for Amber's arrest after hearing Mrs. Carter's story, but then Mr. Carter showed up at the police station with his own version.

He said that his wife had been under a lot of pressure lately and wasn't really responsible for what she'd said. Then he told the police that, at the time in question, they'd actually been having a late dinner at The Steak Place, a fancy new restaurant on the other side of town.

Obviously, she couldn't have been in two places at once! The police checked with restaurant staff, who confirmed that the Carters had been there from shortly after six until almost seven-thirty.

If you can believe the gossip about what happened next, the police went to see Mrs. Carter and gave her a stern warning about false statements and told her she could have been facing criminal charges. But in the end they just let her off. I wondered how she was going to show her face around town after lying and getting caught, and all for five hundred dollars!

It made me shudder when I thought of how easily Amber could have been tried and convicted on a lie. I still didn't know what to think about the whole thing myself, but I sure wouldn't want to see someone go to jail on an invented story.

By Wednesday she was back at school, but there was something really different about her. She was still basically ignoring everyone, but it was with a totally new attitude. Before, she had walked with her head up, looking straight ahead. Now her eyes were cast down toward the floor and she seemed almost slumped into herself. Amber's former indifference had taken on a new tone. It was as if she knew that her self-imposed separation from the other kids had changed. It was no longer her choice but theirs. No one wanted anything to do with her. Well, no one but Greg.

At lunchtime he stopped and gobbled down a sandwich with Betts and me, but as soon as he'd finished eating he stood up. I knew where he was going by the quick look he gave me, a look that said he hoped I understood. And I did. I knew he was going to sit with Amber, not because he didn't want to be with me, but because she needed support.

Betts watched incredulously as he made his way over to her usual corner table.

"I can't believe he's doing that," she said, shaking her head. "You'd think that since he works for the Brodericks and all, he'd be more careful about hanging out with the person who just robbed them."

"The Brodericks don't believe Amber is guilty, Betts," I said quickly. "And I don't think it's fair everyone else assumes she did it either. After all, there's no proof."

"What are you talking about? Of course there's proof. The police wouldn't be so sure it was her otherwise." Betts gave me a slow, questioning look and then asked if I thought Amber was innocent.

"I don't know, and neither does anyone else in this room, except for Amber herself," I found myself saying. "And I think Greg is doing the right thing sitting with her. If you or I were in her position, we'd want someone to believe in us too."

"Then why don't you go over there and join them?" Betts smirked. I could see she was sure I'd never take her up on the suggestion.

It was that smirk that gave me the push I needed. With a sudden rush of determination, I stood and picked up the remains of my lunch.

"Come with me," I said, knowing she wouldn't. "She needs friends now more than she ever did before. I know she hasn't been exactly friendly, but there are reasons for that. Give her a chance, Betts."

"No way. And you're crazy if you go over there," Betts hissed angrily. "You'll be in the same spot she's in. No one will want anything to do with you either."

I shrugged as if it didn't matter. The truth was, it mattered a lot. I didn't want to be ostracized, talked about, and ignored by all my friends. But it suddenly mattered more that I had the courage to do what I thought was right, and that was to help someone who was clearly in need.

My legs shook as I made my way across the cafeteria, and I almost turned back. But then I saw Greg. He'd noticed me heading in their direction and he had this enormously proud and happy look on his face.

When I reached the table I couldn't help but wonder how Amber would react to my presence. After all, aside from that one conversation, we'd never spent any time hanging around together.

"Shelby!" Her face lit up, giving me my answer. "I'm so glad to see you."

CHAPTER NINETEEN

The rest of the week was as bad as I'd feared it would be. I knew I'd been added to the gossip at school, but it got even worse than that. For one thing, not only did everyone else stop talking to me — Betts started ignoring me too! I understood why she was doing it and knew it was because she was afraid she'd be treated the same way, but it hurt just the same. After all, Betts and I have been best friends since we were kids.

It was a lonely feeling, walking through the hallways knowing that the whispers and nasty remarks had swollen to include me. I even heard remarks that suggested Amber, Greg, and I were all in it together.

That gave me a taste of what it was like for Amber. With absolutely nothing to back up the statements, I was being called a thief. Of course, Greg was included in those rumours too, but he seemed totally indifferent to the talk. I wished I could feel the same way, but it bothered me a lot. I could hardly wait for the weekend, just to get away from the talk and hostile looks.

But on Friday when I got home from school I found that the whole thing had followed me. There was nowhere I was going to be safe from the gossip.

Mom met me at the door that day with a worried look on her face and told me that the police were there and wanted to talk to me. Stunned, I followed her into the living room, where two officers sat.

"Miss Belgarden." One of them stood and nodded as though it was some kind of social call. His voice was almost jovial. "How are you today?"

"Fine," I mumbled, feeling a huge lump growing inside me. What could they possibly want with me?

"We just have a few questions to ask you," the other officer, who hadn't bothered to stand, said. His tone wasn't the least bit friendly.

"What kind of questions?" Mom was still beside me, and I wished she'd leave. I couldn't ask her, though, because that would make it look as though there was something I wanted to hide from her.

"Nothing to be alarmed about," the friendly officer said quickly. He turned to face me. "We just wanted to know your whereabouts on Sunday evening, between five and seven o'clock."

"She was here with us," Mom said immediately. There was a mixture of anger and panic in her voice.

"We'd prefer it if Miss Belgarden would answer the questions."

"Why? Do you think my mother is lying?" Even as the angry words came out of my mouth I realized that what my mom had told them wasn't exactly the truth. I was sure she hadn't told a deliberate lie, but the fact was I *hadn't* been home for the whole two hours in question.

"No one is suggesting any such thing," the kindly officer said hastily. "It's just procedure."

My stomach churned. I was debating whether or not I should explain that I'd been out for the afternoon with Greg and had arrived home late for dinner. It had been well past five-thirty when I'd gotten home that night. But if I told them, they'd surely wonder why my mother had said something different.

"So, Miss Belgarden, were you here with your family on Sunday evening between five and seven?"

"Yes." Panic had swept over me, and I couldn't think straight. It seemed best to just agree with what Mom had said. I regretted it the second I'd said it, though, because the hateful officer's eyes lit up as if I'd just given him a huge gift.

"You're sure about that?"

"She answered your question," Mom snapped. I wished she'd stayed quiet.

"Well, that's interesting, because we have two witnesses who place your daughter and another party walking through town between five and five-thirty."

Mom's face changed from anger to fear. She looked
at me as if I'd tricked her somehow, which was hardly
fair considering she was the one who'd been so determined to insist I'd been home.

I tried to explain it then, how I'd been out with
Greg and we'd lost track of the time and it might have
been later than I remembered when I got home for
dinner. My words came out in a jumbled rush, stum-
bling over each other. It sounded as though I was lying,
even to *me*, and I knew it was all true!

That was when the officers said that they'd like to
take me to the police station for a few more questions.
My mom protested, but there seemed nothing to do but
go with them. She was getting her jacket to come along
when my father came in from work. His face turned serious as Mom quickly explained what was happening.

"I'll go with Shelby," he told Mom. "You call our
lawyer and have her meet us at the police station."

Our lawyer? I didn't even known we *had* a lawyer.
And I certainly didn't think I needed one. But I said
nothing and began to follow the police to their waiting
car, which they'd parked out of sight around the corner.
I figured they didn't want to alert me that they were
there, in case I took off like some big criminal. Dad

stopped me and told me to come with him, which I could see annoyed the officers.

To my utter amazement, Dad stopped at a drive-through and ordered us cheeseburgers and fries on the way.

"Eat up," he said calmly. "Who knows how long we'll be tied up with this nonsense, and neither one of us has had our dinner."

Food was the last thing on my mind and I was sure I could never eat a bite, but I stuck a fry in my mouth to be polite and found I was suddenly ravenous. I guess nervousness can make you really hungry sometimes.

We finished eating and then drove to the police station. The two officers looked really annoyed when Dad explained why we were late getting there.

"Can't have the little one starving," Dad said smoothly. His cool, unperturbed manner was starting to calm me too. "Besides, we'll be waiting for Ms. Hill to get here before we begin."

"Well, that's up to you, of course. But I think you should know we have the other party here as well. If anyone wants to cut a deal, it's strictly first come first serve."

Other party? I realized he meant Greg and wondered if he was here alone or if his father was with him. I sure wouldn't have wanted to be facing this without my dad!

Ms. Hill arrived about fifteen minutes after us, and I was astonished at the way she breezed in, looking for all the world as if she was delighted to be there. I'd have thought a lawyer should look a bit more solemn, but she smiled and chatted briefly with everyone before telling the police she wanted a few moments alone with her client.

Apparently, that was me! I went with her into a small room with a wooden table and four chairs.

"Okay, Shelby, we're going to talk to the police in a couple of minutes. Here are the rules. You let me speak at all times. Answer nothing, say nothing. Got it?"

"I didn't do anything wrong," I blurted, surprised that she hadn't even asked me that.

"Yes, well, good then." The way she said that sounded as if it was the least important thing in the world to her. I guess everyone claims they're innocent, so maybe she didn't tend to put much stock in such remarks.

"I really didn't!"

She smiled at me then and there was a twinkle in her eyes. "This has very little to do with guilt or innocence, my dear. What's happening is that the police are conducting an investigation. For whatever reason, they think you may be involved in a crime. Our job is to make sure we don't help them."

"I already told them the truth," I said bitterly. "They just don't believe me."

"Well, this is the way things are, sugar. They're trying to get a case together. To do that, they need to build up evidence. You could say the most innocent thing in the world, which could then be turned around to sound as if you're guilty. That's why you let me talk. They're gathering evidence, and we sure as shootin' aren't going to provide them with any."

A moment later we were all seated around a bigger table in another room.

"Well, boys," Ms. Hill tossed a smile around the room, "I've had a chance to speak to my client. She has no knowledge or involvement in this matter. And that's about it."

"We have a few questions for Miss Belgarden," one of the officers said dismally. It seemed he knew what was coming next.

"And you know, we'd love to help you out, but as I said, my client doesn't know a darned thing." Another smile, accompanied by what seemed to be a helpless shrug. "Naturally, in light of that, I've advised Miss Belgarden not to talk to you. Nor will you attempt to speak with her at any time in the future unless I am present."

"I think you should know that we're questioning another youth at this time," the other officer said threateningly. "We can only offer a deal to one of these young people, so if he speaks first, your client is out of luck."

Rather than looking worried over this, Ms. Hill laughed right out loud and said, "Well, I sure hope he has an attorney. You boys are obviously grasping at straws, so we'll be off now."

She stood and snapped up her briefcase. Dad and I followed her to the parking lot. Our feet had barely landed on the pavement when she whirled around to face me.

"This other kid, is there anything, and I mean *anything*, he might tell them that would suggest either of you are involved in this thing?"

"No! We're *not* involved!" I was shocked at the question, considering how confident she'd seemed only seconds ago. Now it looked as if she doubted me.

"Excellent! That's what I thought, kiddo, but I have to ask." She patted my arm, told Dad to call any time we needed her, and hurried off.

Dad put his arm around my shoulders and gave me a squeeze.

"Let's go home and calm down your poor mother."

CHAPTER TWENTY

When we got back home, Mom threw her arms around me and went on and on about her "poor baby."

"How could they do this to you?" she almost sobbed. She told us that the few hours we'd been gone had seemed like days and that she'd been losing her mind with worry.

"Now, now, there's nothing to worry about, dear," Dad said, putting his arms around the two of us. "Shelby has promised me that she's going to give up her life of crime."

"That's not funny, Randall!"

I giggled, but inside I was worried about Greg. I'd heard that the police are allowed to lie in order to trick people into confessions. What if they told Greg I had said something about him? Would he know they were making it up?

My fears were allayed a few hours later when he showed up at our house.

"Looking for your partner in crime, are you?" I heard my father's voice at the door.

I flew down the hallway and gave Dad a quick poke in the ribs, just to let him know I'd heard what he'd said. Then I hugged Greg, not caring who was watching.

"Hey." His smile made my insides all mush. "I just came by to see if you were all right. I understand they brought you in for questioning too."

I told him about my experience with the police and how Ms. Hill had stopped them cold. Greg seemed impressed at that, and admitted that he had given them a statement.

"I hope it wasn't a mistake," he said reflectively. "I assumed that if I cooperated they'd know I had nothing to hide. But it sounds as if your lawyer wouldn't agree with what I did."

"What I can't figure out is why they wanted to talk to *us*."

"Guilt by association, I guess. They must have learned that you and I are Amber's friends. Or they might think she probably told us something and that treating us like suspects too would make us rat her out."

I sighed. "It's already been hard enough at school without this. When word gets around that we were taken in for questioning things will only get worse."

"And we're still just on the sidelines of this whole thing," Greg pointed out softly. "Think of what it's like for Amber. She's the one who's affected the most."

I knew he was right, but a part of me was starting to resent her for all the trouble. It wasn't fair or reasonable to feel that way, but I couldn't help it. I almost wished I'd never even heard the name Amber Chapman. I found it hard to sympathize with her position, especially since I wasn't fully convinced of her innocence. I needed evidence one way or the other.

That thought gave me an idea.

"Where's your dad tonight?"

"He was in town getting groceries when I got home from school. In fact, he doesn't even know about what happened this evening, since he wasn't there when the police came and picked me up. I didn't want to alarm him so I just left a note saying I'd be back soon."

"I want to talk to him." Dr. Taylor is a psychologist and he'd been helpful to me before. "Can we go to your place?"

"Sure, if you want to."

I went to tell Mom and Dad (who'd miraculously given us some privacy) where I was going, and then slipped on my jacket and shoes.

It was a cold evening and we walked quickly. As we were turning down the street Greg lives on he stopped and turned toward me.

"You'd think a guy could get a kiss after going through a brutal police interrogation."

I was only too happy to comply. His nose was cold on my face, but I didn't mind.

"You know, that wasn't very thoughtful of me," he said afterward. "After all, you've just been through the same trauma. You probably need comfort too."

"I do," I nodded solemnly. "I know I had a lawyer and all, but she called me things like 'sugar' and 'kiddo.' It was *awful*." In fact, I'd liked her friendly way of talking, but telling him that wasn't going to get me anywhere.

"How you must have suffered." His lips were on mine then, and I can truly say I felt adequately comforted.

"Were the police really brutal to you?" I asked after we'd resumed walking.

"Actually, they were pretty decent. I guess they were just doing their jobs." He smiled. "I suppose you want your kiss back now that you know I got it under false pretences."

I would have liked to say yes, but we were in sight of his house by then and that made me feel shy. I told him I'd let him off this time, but he'd better watch himself from now on. He didn't seem too alarmed.

Dr. Taylor was in the book room, reading an old-looking volume called *Horace Walpole's England*. He set it aside and listened with interest as we told him what had happened to us that evening.

"It does sound as though they're digging for something solid against Amber," Dr. Taylor said when we'd finished filling him in. "Unfortunately, as long as their investigation is focused in her direction, there's a danger that they'll overlook things that may point to someone else."

"That's why I wanted to talk to you," I told him. "I was wondering what kind of person would commit a robbery like that."

"From a psychological point of view?" He nodded. "Well, I appreciate the compliment of you asking me, but I don't know how much help I can be. People steal for different reasons, so they don't fall into a nice, tidy category."

"What reason would someone have for stealing, aside from the fact that they want something?"

"It's a mistake to think people steal primarily to obtain something. In fact, that's one of the less common reasons. And those are generally crimes of impulse, where they see an item they want and grab it. A planned theft has a deeper purpose. A robbery is planned out, and the objective is clearly money."

"So, the thefts at school would be impulsive?"

"I wouldn't say that either. They needed a certain amount of planning too, making sure no one was around, finding out where particular items were kept and so on. No, I'd say that the thief at your school had a purpose in mind. If the items that were taken all had value, it's likely they were sold to obtain cash.

"I think the question you're really asking is *why* this person is stealing," he continued. "And you've decided that the thefts at school and the robbery were committed by the same person."

"It seems likely," I agreed. "After all, the gas station holdup happened right after the thefts at school. Everyone had started being really careful, not leaving things in their lockers and stuff. I think whoever is doing it ran out of things to steal at school because of all the increased caution and that's when he or she decided to rob Broderick's."

"Sounds like an act of desperation. One source dried up, so another had to be found." He nodded. "If you're right in your theory that we're talking about a single culprit, then we can rule out mental disorders like kleptomania."

"Why?"

"Because kleptomaniacs steal *things*, they don't rob stores."

"So, the thief is only interested in money or things that can be sold for money!"

"I'd say that's a safe bet. And in that case, you're

probably looking for a person who needs money for a particular reason."

"Such as?"

"Well, for example, drug addicts steal to pay for their habits. Or someone who is poor may develop an obsession to have money to buy things he or she can't afford otherwise. The same would go for a person whose financial circumstances are suddenly reduced and who can't accept a change in lifestyle."

"So there's no actual common trait in thieves?"

"Not in the way you're asking, although it's impossible to find a thief who isn't also a liar. You see, stealing fosters lies. On the other hand, lots of people lie but don't steal, so that's not an accurate guideline."

We chatted a bit longer, but Dr. Taylor didn't have a whole lot to add to what he'd told me. Still, I was sure he'd said something helpful, although I couldn't quite put my finger on what it was.

CHAPTER TWENTY-ONE

I spent the rest of the weekend just hanging around the house. Greg was working extra shifts because old man Broderick didn't want Amber there until things had settled down a bit. I think he figured people might give her a hard time.

It's not that I couldn't have gone somewhere if I'd wanted, but I knew the whole town would have heard that Greg and I had been questioned by the police. The stares and muffled whispers at school were bad enough without getting the same thing from everyone in Little River. I kept wondering how long it was going to go on.

Mom told me I should just hold my head up and ignore what people were saying, but that's easier said than done. And no matter how much I told myself it would soon blow over, I knew that if the robbery wasn't solved the rumours could follow me around forever.

I have to admit that the whole thing got me think-ing hard about Amber. She already had a lot to deal with, considering the situation with her family and all. Being accused of stealing and having her new commu-nity judge her must be making her life a total misery. Of course, that's assuming she really was innocent.

On Sunday afternoon I called her and asked her if she wanted to come over for a while, maybe stay for dinner. Her voice sounded really down, and though she thanked me for the invitation, she said that she didn't feel much like going anywhere. I knew how she felt.

One thing I noticed was that our phone rang a whole lot more than it normally did over the weekend. It wasn't hard to tell, from the things Mom said on the phone, that the callers were hoping to get some infor-mation. That really made me furious. My mom has never been a gossip, and there she was stuck dealing with all these nosy people and trying to be polite about it. A couple of times she got exasperated and told callers that she was busy, ending the conversations with a curt goodbye and hanging up. I figured they'd gone too far and had asked something really impertinent, but Mom wouldn't talk about what had been said.

Greg told me on Monday morning that it was the busiest weekend he'd ever had at work. It seemed that everyone in town needed gas.

"I got so sick of answering questions," he sighed. "Some people even came right out and asked me if you and I were suspects. Others just looked really surprised that I was still working there, as if I'd been tried and convicted and they couldn't understand why Mr. Broderick hadn't fired me."

I hadn't thought things could get any worse at school, but I was dead wrong about that.

A lot of kids were openly hostile, and a few came right up to me and made nasty remarks. Others seemed embarrassed and avoided looking at me. I figured they felt sorry for me and might have liked to say something kind or helpful, but were afraid to.

The principal, Mr. Lower, gave a talk over the PA system that was a lot like the one he'd given me in his office the day I'd accused Amber of stealing my watch. I know he meant to help, but all it did was draw more attention to the whole thing. While he talked about being careful not to judge a person without all the facts, several of my classmates snorted and muttered things that were less than complimentary. My face burned, and I must have looked as guilty as could be.

At lunchtime I could hardly force myself to eat my sandwich. It felt like cardboard in my mouth and tasted about the same. It amazed me that Greg seemed so unaffected, laughing and talking as if everything was perfectly normal. Amber, on the other hand, seemed to be having the same trouble I was. After a few attempts to eat she pushed her lunch aside without managing more than a couple of bites.

"How can you be so cheerful?" I asked Greg.

"Easy. I just keep imagining how much fun it's going to be when everyone finds out they were wrong."

"Fun? In what way?" Amber looked curious.

"Think about it," he smiled. "Once the real culprit is caught, the kids who've been making snide remarks and acting like jerks are going to have to face what they did. Don't you think it's going to be embarrassing for them to realize they treated us that way for no reason?"

"I guess. But that's only *if* the police catch the person who actually did it."

"They *will*. And then the three of us will be in a position to show how gracious and forgiving we are, which will only add to their embarrassment."

But it turned out that our tiny group of outcasts was about to increase from three to four. A moment after Greg's remark, I glanced up and saw Betts standing beside the table. She took a deep breath and plunked herself down in an empty chair.

"Hey, Betts," I said, as if her joining us was a perfectly normal occurrence.

"Hey, Shelb." Betts's voice was soft and awkward. I knew she'd probably been feeling as bad as I had over the way things had been for the past week.

"Betts, this is Amber. Amber, Betts." Greg spoke up quickly. The girls nodded to each other, but they both looked uncomfortable.

"Betts, you're Shelby's best friend, aren't you?" Amber asked hesitantly.

"We've been best friends forever." Betts seemed surprised by the fact that Amber was making conversation. I also noticed that her answer sounded much like a question and that she was looking toward me as she spoke. I suppose that she wondered if her recent actions had changed things between us.

"That's right," I chimed in quickly. "Betts and I go way back."

Amber smiled and nodded, but then her face got a sad, faraway look. I realized she must be thinking about her friends back in Alberta.

That night as I was getting ready to go to sleep I tried to picture what it had all been like for Amber. I thought of how it would feel to have my mom tell me that I was too much trouble and that she was sending me off to live with relatives I barely even knew. A jumble of emotions rushed in on me as I imagined what it would be like. Packing my clothes, wondering when, if ever, I'd see my home and family again. Saying good-bye to my friends, leaving behind everything familiar and going to a strange place. It was horrible just thinking about it. And Amber had lived it.

As I drifted off to sleep I said a little prayer that things would get better.

Over the next week it began to look as though my prayer was being answered. After Betts joined us in the cafeteria that day, other students started coming around. Annie Berkley was the next one to make a move. I was heading down the hallway after school when she approached me.

"Hi, Shelby."

"Hi, Annie."

"Things sure are weird here these days." Her normally ruddy complexion was even redder than usual.

"Yeah, they're pretty strange all right."

"Well, I just wanted you to know that I don't believe all the stories."

"Thanks."

"I haven't forgotten how you and your dad took up for me that time Kelsey made fun of me at the Scream Machine."

"It was a rotten thing for her to do," I said, remembering the incident.

"The way everyone is treating you lately is worse, though." She bit her lower lip, which she always does when she's nervous. "Anyway, I'm sorry I haven't said anything before now."

"That's okay, Annie. I know it's not easy." Boy, did I ever know!

From that point on, a few other kids started talking to me again. Most of them just acted like they'd never given me the silent treatment at all. It was as if the last week and a half had never happened. That was okay with me.

There was one thing that wasn't okay. Even though some of the students were talking to me and Betts and Greg again, the shifting attitude didn't include Amber.

I understood how hurt she'd been when was sent to Little River, and why that would make her so determined to shut everyone out, but she sure hadn't done herself any favours. In trying to protect herself from any more hurt, she'd become an easy target for gossip and antagonism.

Amber's attitude was changing, though. She seemed to realize that she needed friends, no matter how betrayed she'd been in the past. Because of the shift in her outlook, I think the other students would eventually have come around and accepted her, in spite of everything.

But then something else happened, and instead of things continuing to get better, they got a whole lot worse.

Chapter Twenty-Two

The next big event in Little River took place on a Thursday night, though no one knew anything about it until Friday morning.

I'd just wandered sleepily into the kitchen and was about to sit down for breakfast when I heard sirens blaring in the distance. The sound sent a chill through me, even though I had no reason to think it was going to affect me. If you've been dragged to the police station and questioned about a crime, you tend to get a bit nervous about sirens.

It wasn't long before I heard that Samuels' Music Store had been broken into. Apparently, the thief had made off with the money from the cash register. Whether or not anything else was missing wouldn't be known until Mr. Samuels had a chance to do a complete inventory.

Greg and Amber and I had gone to the Scream Machine and a movie that Thursday evening, so when I heard there'd been a robbery I figured we were all safe. At least, we had an alibi up until around eleven o'clock, which was late for me to be allowed out on a school night. I'd been all ready to beg, but Mom surprised me and said I could go as soon as I asked her.

We'd walked Amber home and then gone to my place, where Greg called his dad to come and pick him up. I thought it was a lucky coincidence that we'd passed the music store on our way home and had stopped to look at a poster in the window that was announcing a contest for a trip to meet your favourite rock star. Everything had been quiet and there was no sign of a break-in then, so the robbery must have taken place later on, when the three of us would all have been safely home.

Of course that was the big topic at school that morning and I felt strangely glad it had happened. After all, since Amber had been with me and Greg, they couldn't accuse her of this one. That would get the police looking somewhere else for the culprit. I figured it would help clear Amber of the gas station robbery too, assuming the same person had committed both crimes.

I got home from school at the usual time and was happy to find a letter from my friend Jane on the kitchen table. It was upbeat and cheerful, except for a part about her group meetings. And that wasn't really bad either, though it was sad to read. It showed that she was really making progress in dealing with what had happened to her.

The survivor's group has been a great help to me. Just knowing that I'm not the only one who's been through this makes it easier. Besides, I can talk about anything and no one is shocked. We were talking the other day about mothers and I asked why a mother wouldn't automatically know that something was wrong with her child. It seems to me that my mom should have realized what was going on, even if I didn't say anything to her.

Then Crystal, another girl in the group, said that was the hardest thing for her too. She said most mothers would do anything they had to do to protect their children, and she felt her mom had just totally failed her. We both started crying then, and so did most of the other kids in the group. Afterward, I felt a lot better. Being able to say what I'd felt for so long and letting it out like that really helped a lot.

I decided to answer Jane's letter right away and was just about to go to my room for writing paper when the doorbell rang. Mom called out from the other room for to me to see who it was, but before I opened the door I already knew. I'd glimpsed the white vehicle with flashing lights through the side window.

"Mom, it's the police," I yelled as I reached for the doorknob.

"Afternoon, Miss Belgarden," one said courteously after I'd pulled the door open. They stepped into the kitchen just as Mom hurried into the room.

"We have a few questions for your daughter, ma'am." The same officer who'd greeted me turned to Mom. "Would you prefer that we interview her here or at the station?"

"It doesn't matter where you interview me," I said quickly. "My lawyer has told me not to answer any questions."

"You've already spoken to a lawyer about the incident last evening?" The other officer spoke this time. He sounded surprised and a little suspicious. "Why would you have done that?"

"No, it was about the robbery at the gas station," I answered, realizing these two hadn't been involved then. "But I'm sure she'd give me the same advice about this. And anyway, I have an alibi for last night."

"An *alibi*?" his eyebrows were raised and I knew

right away that had been the wrong thing to say. I guess an innocent person doesn't automatically mention an alibi when the police show up at the door.

"I mean, I was with some friends all evening. We didn't have anything to do with the break-in at the music store."

"So, you and your friends weren't anywhere near Samuels'?"

I swallowed hard. "I think I want to call my lawyer," I told him.

"Well, of course you can do that, if you feel you *need* a lawyer," his voice was smooth, but there was an undercurrent that made me nervous.

Mom was looking back and forth between us. Her face was scared.

"What exactly did you want to know?" she asked slowly. "It's not as though Shelby has anything to hide."

"I'm sure she doesn't, but if she's not willing to talk to us ..." his voice trailed off in a way that implied he thought I *did* have something to hide. Then he added, "We're following up on some reports, and we'd just like to clear a few things up."

"Maybe you should just answer their questions," Mom told me. "I'm sure that will be the end of it."

I wished Dad was there, but he wouldn't be home for at least another hour. I was sure he'd have called Ms.

Hill instead of suggesting I go ahead and talk to the police. It was true that I had nothing to hide. At the same time, I knew I'd somehow become a suspect, and if I talked to the police, anything that came out wrong could easily be misinterpreted.

Still, it would look bad if I refused to answer their questions after my own mother had told me to go ahead. I felt trapped.

So, we sat down in the living room and they asked me about the night before. Where had I been, what movie did we see, what time did we leave the theatre, where had we gone afterward?

I did my best to be careful when I answered them. I went over the evening bit by bit, telling them everything I could remember. I almost didn't mention stopping at Samuels' on the way home, worried that that would look suspicious. In the end, I did tell them that, and I was glad I had because one of the officers nodded in a way that made me sure someone had seen us and told the police we'd been there.

They took turns talking to me, and repeated some of the questions two and even three times. Finally, Mom pointed out that I'd cooperated and answered everything and that she saw no reason to keep asking me things over and over.

That was when one of the officers reached into his case and took out a couple of pictures. "Miss

Belgarden, have you ever seen this key chain before?"

I looked at the first picture, which he'd handed to me. The photo was of an oval-shaped, gold-coloured key chain with an eagle etched onto it. I shook my head and told him I didn't remember ever seeing it before.

Then he handed me the other picture, which he identified as being the other side of the key chain. I saw that there was an inscription on it, and panic rose in me as I read it.

"To A. C. Love Grandma."

CHAPTER TWENTY-THREE

"Come on, Shelby, what do any of us really know about Amber?"

I hated to admit that Betts was right, but she was. None of us knew much about the girl who'd come to Little River. I probably knew more than anyone else, but then, I had no way of being sure that the things she'd told me were even true.

Still, I rose to her defence and pointed out that the evidence against her was all circumstantial.

"How much more do you need?" Betts's voice was exasperated, and I could see that her patience was growing thin. "The gas station is robbed when she's on duty. There are no witnesses, except the guy who was there just before the robbery who said she was gone for a while. That gave her the perfect opportunity to hide the money before she called the police with a story about being held up. Then the three of you stop at Samuels' on your way from the show and it just happens to get robbed later that night. And her key chain is found on the floor there!"

"Amber says it's not her key chain," I said lamely.

"Right. It just happens to have her initials on it, but it's not hers."

"But the key didn't fit the lock on the Brodericks' house."

"So what? It's probably a key from somewhere else she's lived. I don't know why you're so determined to believe she's innocent. It's almost as if you'd have to catch her in the act before you'd see that she's guilty."

I was glad I hadn't told Betts about the incident at school when Amber had put my watch in her pocket!

The truth was, my own belief in Amber was shaken. It seemed that the case against her just kept getting stronger and stronger.

"You're not keeping an open mind," Betts accused.

"Maybe I'm not," I said slowly. "But after getting to know Amber a little bit, I just feel sure she couldn't have done those things."

Betts rolled her eyes, which is what she always does when she's decided I'm being hopeless. "Well, someone did. And that someone has the initials A.C."

"We don't know that for sure either," I said stubbornly. "The key chain could have been there before the robbery."

"Mr. Samuels says he swept up after closing that night and there was nothing on the floor."

I didn't bother arguing anymore, mainly because I was losing and knew there was no chance of changing that.

The situation at school had been bad enough before the robbery at the music store. After that occurrence it turned outright hostile. No one wanted to talk to anyone who associated with Amber Chapman. At that point this only included Greg and me, since Betts had switched back to her previous attitude. I could see her point in not wanting to be ostracized and didn't hold it against her.

By Tuesday of the next week, Amber had been arrested and charged for both robberies. I guess the police figured they had enough evidence for a conviction. Amber wasn't at school the rest of that week, which actually took a little pressure off Greg and me. At first I thought she must be in jail somewhere, but that wasn't the case. She'd been charged and released until her trial, which was two months away. Greg told me the Brodericks had insisted that she take a few days off school.

"That almost makes her look guilty," I remarked.

"Heck, I hope that doesn't turn everyone who thinks she's innocent against her," he said sarcastically. He had a point there. It wasn't as if the general opinion about her was going to be affected by her absence from class. Everyone already thought she was guilty.

The police wanted to question me again, but Dad was home that time and told them to contact my lawyer instead. He hadn't been too happy to learn that Mom had already let me talk to them, a sentiment that Ms. Hill shared. She called me up and gave me a raking for not following her advice. When I pointed out that my mother had told me to answer their questions, she remarked that *she* was my lawyer and that if I wanted my mom to represent me instead I should just let her know.

I felt properly chastised although I didn't really think I was to blame in the whole matter. Still, there's no arguing with a woman like Ms. Hill. To tell the truth, I was glad to have someone like her taking care of the whole mess for me.

Greg was working a lot on the weekends, which left me without much to look forward to, especially since Betts had become reluctant to spend any time with me. I knew she felt bad about it but just didn't have the courage to stand by me, at least not so far as everyone else knew. I was sure that everything would get back to normal between us once this whole thing blew over. In the meantime, days off school were pretty boring.

I decided to go over to the Brodericks' to see Amber on Saturday. I went without calling first just in case she tried to put me off. She might not have felt like seeing anyone, but that didn't mean she didn't *need* to.

Old man Broderick met me at the door and welcomed me in with a big smile. Amber was in the kitchen making cookies with Mrs. Broderick. The way her face lit up when she saw me made me glad I was there.

"Shelby! I didn't know you were coming over."

"Well, I heard there were cookies being made." The aroma of chocolate chips filled the house and made me suddenly hungry.

"Rita is the best cook in the world," Mr. Broderick's voice came from behind me. I hadn't realized he'd followed me into the kitchen.

"Aw now, Earl," Mrs. Broderick demurred, but she looked pleased with her husband's compliment.

"She tried to hide a cake from me once," he smiled at the memory, "but I found it. Just followed my trusty nose to the cupboard in the porch."

Before I could wonder why Mrs. Broderick would be hiding food from her husband she explained that the cake had been for a Ladies' Auxiliary bake sale. It wasn't until she went to add it to the other items on display that she discovered her beautiful cake was missing several pieces. Mr. Broderick looked supremely satisfied with himself as his wife retold the story.

Amber and I giggled, mostly because of the expression on his face. Mrs. Broderick shook her head and said what a rascal he'd been, but her words were belied by the fact that she was smiling too.

There's something awfully sweet about an old couple who still obviously love each other. That's the way the Brodericks are, and it made me glad that Amber was living with them. With everything else that was going on in her life, she at least had a happy home to go to every day.

When the cookies were all baked and the kitchen cleaned, Amber and I went out to the backyard swing, where we sat talking and eating cookies.

"You must be pretty nervous about the trial and all," I said sympathetically.

"It's like a nightmare." Her voice was low and trembled slightly. "I keep thinking they'll realize the whole thing is a mistake, but there's no sign of that happening. I don't know what will happen to me if they find me guilty."

"They won't!" I assured her with more confidence than I felt.

"You know what the worst thing is?" Tears were forming in her eyes. "My own mother doesn't even believe me. She thinks I did it as some kind of rebellion for being sent away."

"You were talking to your mom?" I was surprised.

"The police called her about the key. Of course the one they found at the music store won't match any keys we've ever had, because it's *not mine*, but I doubt that will make any difference. They'll just think my mother is trying to protect me."

"Did they call your dad too?"

"Probably. I haven't heard from him, though. Maybe he thinks I'm guilty too and is ashamed to talk to me."

When I left, just before dinner, my certainty in Amber's innocence had been restored. Her worry over the trial and the anguish she showed over her mom's reaction were too sincere. There was no way a guilty person could put on an act that convincingly.

It was equally clear to me that with so much circumstantial evidence pointing in her direction, the only way that she was going to be cleared was if the real felon was found. And since the police were satisfied that Amber was the culprit, they weren't looking for anyone else.

It was at that point that the feeling came to me that the answer was right under my nose. There was something I was missing.

I had to figure out what it was.

CHAPTER TWENTY-FOUR

It's funny how when you try to think of something it runs off and you can't get it to the surface. It was like that with me on the whole matter of the robberies. The more I concentrated and tried to force myself to bring up whatever was lurking in my brain, the more it seemed to hide from me.

I went over and over the details I knew about Broderick's and Samuels', but there was nothing that popped out as significant. Nothing that would point to the guilty person. Instead, everything seemed to fall in with the police theory that Amber was guilty. I could certainly see why Betts thought I was crazy for continuing to believe in her when all the facts suggested she was the culprit.

The thefts at school had started shortly after her arrival in Little River too. I had the nagging feeling that that really didn't support the idea of her guilt, but couldn't figure out why. There was something that was eluding me.

Then I was washing dishes after dinner on Sunday, not thinking of anything in particular, when a jumble of thoughts began running through my head.

Think. Think about the thefts that *didn't* happen at school.

Amber's remark about the key. *They'll just think my mother is trying to protect me.*

Betts's comment about the key chain. *Well someone did. And that someone has the initials A.C.*

Dr. Taylor's words. *Drug addicts steal to pay for their habits.*

None of these things seemed the least bit helpful. It was just a conglomeration of unrelated things that didn't even fit together.

The last thought was most perplexing of all. Little River High had a huge anti-drug campaign a few years ago, when drug use had begun to be a serious problem. It was actually started by a group of students who were worried about their friends. Guest speakers came to both the middle and high schools. A two-day event was held where information was presented and students were asked to sign a contract promising to stay drug- and alcohol-free.

Most of us signed the contract and kept our commitment. Posters were put up everywhere, and students painted huge murals with drug-free themes in hallways all over the school. My favourite one is a dark scene with a ghostly figure slumped in a dark alley. Over the top it says "Users are Losers."

The schools and the community started holding special events where anyone who was suspected of using wasn't allowed in, or got thrown out. Before long, it was the users who were in the minority. Peer pressure became a powerful tool as it got behind the idea and swelled.

The schools both adopted a zero tolerance policy on drugs. Anyone who was found using or carrying on school property had a five-day suspension for the first offence and a suspension for the rest of the school year for a second offence. If a student was suspected of being high in class, parents were called and informed of the school's concern.

Every once in a while the police dog, Spotter, came for a "visit." It wasn't long before students realized that they might be able to hide drugs from everyone else, but they couldn't hide anything from Spotter. He's amazing. I've seen a few panic-stricken faces in the hallways when he'd appear, padding along beside his human co-officer. When he'd smell something, he'd stop suddenly and bark, his tail sticking straight out behind him. Whether he was standing in front of a student, a locker, or a bookbag, someone was busted!

Spotter did more to help clean things up than everything else put together.

Of course, there are still a few potheads around, but in general the campaign was incredibly effective.

So, you can see that the idea that the robberies might be drug related didn't make sense. I couldn't figure out why that thought had come along with the others, but then I didn't see the connection of the other things either. Probably, none of it had any significance or importance. It certainly didn't give me any ideas about who had committed the crimes.

Still, when I'd finished the dishes I got a sheet of paper out and made a list:

Think about the thefts that *didn't* happen
at school.

I felt silly writing that one. What help would it be to think about something that hadn't even occurred? And for that matter, how could I possibly know what the thief might have tried to take and couldn't, for one reason or another?

The key. The police will think Amber's mother
is protecting her?
Someone with the initials A. C.
Drug addicts steal to support their habits.

I felt a bit foolish when I read back over the list. "There's nothing here that means anything at all," I said aloud.

You're missing something.

The thought that I was missing something came like an accusation. It was so frustrating! I almost crumpled up the paper and threw it in the garbage, but on the off chance that even one item on the list actually meant something, I put it in my room instead.

Greg wasn't working Sunday night, though he'd been on the job most of the weekend. He'd mentioned that he had a paper to finish writing for English class, so I knew he'd be home working on that. After arguing with myself over whether or not it was fair to disturb him when he had so little time to get his assignment done, I picked up the phone and dialed his number.

He answered on the fourth ring, which increased my guilt.

"Greg, I'm sorry to bother you when you've got homework to do."

"Don't ever apologize for calling me," he laughed. "I love … hearing from you."

My heart did a little flip-flop. Could he have been about to say he loved me? It almost made me forget why I was calling.

"Anyway, the paper's almost done. I've been writing it in my head all weekend, at work. Now it's just a matter of putting it on paper."

"I wanted to talk to you about Amber."

"Sure. What's up? Is there something new?"

"Not exactly, but there were some things that came into my head a while ago and I just can't seem to make sense of them. I thought maybe if I talked to you, you might have some ideas."

Then I went over the list of things I'd written. They sounded even sillier than ever.

"Okay, so what you have are bits of information that don't *seem* to be related, right?"

I agreed that was the case.

"But they must mean *something*. Obviously, you've been spending time thinking about the whole robbery situation. I think you should look at your list as clues. Even if the things you've written down aren't related to each other, they're probably all somehow related to the robberies."

"But how?"

"I don't know. But it's in your head, and you must be getting somewhere with it, even if you feel that you're not. I'd say just relax and let other thoughts come out; keep writing them down. It's like a puzzle, and you've got some of the pieces there. You just need more to get the whole picture."

I felt encouraged by that. Then he made another suggestion.

"You know, babe, the robberies all happened within the last few months. Maybe it would help to write down everything you can remember that happened during that time period. Even things that don't seem related in any way. Something might jump out at you that you'd otherwise overlook or miss."

It seemed like a big job, and one that would probably be a waste of time. In spite of that, I got out a couple of notebooks, one for each month, and began to jot down notes.

After all, two months was not such a long time. And that was how much time Amber had left before her trial.

Chapter Twenty-Five

Amber was back at school on Monday. By the end of the day she looked absolutely defeated. From the short time I'd spent with her in the cafeteria, I knew what she'd endured. It was as if there was a sphere of tension surrounding her, penetrated by regular comments from the other students. I heard the word "thief" tossed in her direction a few times, and the glares of hostility were impossible to ignore.

"I don't think I can handle this much longer," she whispered to me in the schoolyard when classes had been let out for the afternoon. "Everyone hates me."

"They don't hate *you*, Amber. They hate what *they think* you did. Once they find out they were wrong, things will get better."

My words didn't seem to cheer her much, even though she made an effort to smile.

"And when do you suppose that will happen?" Her voice was flat and emotionless as she asked this, as though she had little interest in the answer.

I wanted to promise her it would be soon, that this would all be over and she could look forward to a normal life. Instead, I admitted that I didn't know.

My heart was heavy as I watched her walk away. She looked so alone and lost, a tiny form making its way through a town that had judged her.

"I don't suppose I might get to spend a little time with my girlfriend this evening."

Turning, I saw Greg standing behind me.

"Oh, Greg. We have to *do* something."

"That's what I was suggesting."

"I mean about Amber. She's really down. I'm worried about her."

"Now that sounds like a romantic evening." His teasing remark was betrayed by the cloud of concern in his eyes.

Consider the timing.

I must have looked startled as this odd thought popped into my head because Greg leaned forward slightly, a question on his face.

"I just had a strange thought," I explained. "It came out of nowhere, like the others I had yesterday."

"What was it?"

When I told him, he nodded, as though it was something important.

"Let's take a walk after dinner tonight," he suggested. "Just wander around and relax. Maybe something else will come to you. At the very least, we can talk about the whole thing."

I agreed, glad at the thought of being out of the house. It seemed I'd been indoors almost constantly in the past week.

He arrived to pick me up at six o'clock, while Mom and I were doing the dishes.

"I'll just be a few minutes," I told him, but Mom insisted that she'd finish up herself.

I grabbed my jacket and we headed out, walking aimlessly through town. Before long I was thirsty, and we stopped to get bottles of water at the One Stop convenience store.

"You two are friends of that crook, aren't you?" the woman behind the counter asked accusingly. Her hands clasped her blouse nervously, as if she was afraid we were going to pull out a gun and rob her.

"No, ma'am," Greg said politely. "We *are* friends of the girl who was charged, but she's innocent."

"You *say*," she sniffed. "You think her parents sent her here for no reason? I bet she was in trouble with the law where she came from."

"We didn't come in here to argue," Greg's voice stayed calm and civil. "We just want to make our purchase and leave."

"Make your purchase somewhere else," she snapped. "This is a respectable store, and the likes of you aren't wanted here."

"Our money is as good as anyone's," Greg said softly. His arm slid around my waist, steadying me. The shock of being talked to that way made me feel as though I'd been kicked in the stomach.

"Not everything is about money! There are other things that are more important, like reputation." Her chin rose and she shot us withering looks, as though our very presence was defiling the store. "Now, there's the door. Get out."

Greg shrugged, took the bottles of water back to the cooler and put them back on the shelf. We walked out of the store.

"When this is all cleared up," I said angrily once we were back on the street, "I'm going to go in there and demand an apology."

"An apology that's demanded is hardly ever sincere," he answered. "It would be better to go in and just be nice. That would be more likely to make her feel genuinely sorry and ashamed of the way she treated us."

"How could she talk that way, ordering us out of the store as if we were some kind of criminals?" I seethed. "She doesn't know anything about us."

"It's just fear. People want to protect what's theirs. With all the crazy stories going around, she saw us as some kind of a threat."

"Yeah, we're a *big* threat." I mimicked her nasty words. "Not everything is about money. There are other things more important, like reputation."

"I think she was overreacting there," Greg sighed. "It's not as if our presence in the store was going to ruin the business or anything."

"Well, I don't know how you stayed so calm and polite to the old witch."

"That's because of a simple lesson I learned from my dad," he smiled. "He always told me, never let someone else decide how you're going to act. Anyway, let's talk about something else."

"Okay, but I'm still thirsty."

"Right. Well, if we cross through the back of the bus stop property it will bring us out to Broderick's and we can get you your water there. I don't think he'll throw us out."

So we did, and then continued along. He took my hand as we walked, and before long his calming presence had made me feel better.

"That idea you had earlier, about timing. Have you given it any more thought?"

"Not really," I admitted. "Well, I did think about

when each robbery had taken place, but there's no relation. One was on a Sunday, the other was on a Thursday. Aside from the fact that both happened at night, there doesn't seem to be any real connection."

"Sunday and Thursday," he repeated slowly. "I can't think of anything there either."

We talked about the other things I'd written down, but after reviewing them we were no closer to arriving at any sort of conclusion.

When I got home I added "Timing" to my list of "clues" and looked it all over again. There's something here, I thought, why can't I see what it is?

By the time I got ready for bed that night I was exhausted from straining to think about the whole subject. As I was drifting off to sleep, the last thought that came to me wasn't about the robberies at all, or at least it didn't seem to be. Instead, the woman from the store's words drifted through my head.

"Not everything is about money! There are other things that are more important, like reputation."

It all seemed hopeless.

CHAPTER TWENTY-SIX

It was still partially dark outside when I woke up the next morning. I turned to the clock on my night table and half groaned to see that it was barely past six. For a few minutes I lay there trying to get back to sleep but soon realized that wasn't going to happen. I was vaguely aware that I'd been awakened by a dream. Little snatches of it flitted through my head and I made a futile effort to catch it before it slipped away completely. There was no sense in that, as I well knew. The harder you try to remember a dream, the faster it disappears completely.

I slid out of bed after lying there for about ten minutes, washed up, and got a glass of orange juice from the kitchen. My parents wouldn't be up for nearly an hour so I tiptoed past their door on the way back to my room, careful not to disturb them.

Deciding to read for a while until everyone was out of bed, I went to my desk and glanced at the books on the shelf above it. Then I noticed Jane's last letter sitting beside the lamp and remembered that I still hadn't answered it. This would be a good time to do that.

I always read through a letter while I'm answering it, to make sure I don't miss any questions or forget to comment on anything important. Well, I was halfway through writing when part of a sentence in Jane's letter leapt off the page at me.

"Most mothers would do anything they had to do, to protect their children ..."

Amber had commented that the police would probably think her mother was just protecting her if they didn't match the key they'd found at Samuels' to any of the homes she'd lived in while in Alberta.

Before I had time to consider how these two things related to each other, the words from the lady at the convenience store came rushing back.

"Not everything is about money."

Snatches of conversation and small details I'd not connected with the crimes flashed through my brain. It was like overload, with a burst of thoughts and ideas rushing into my head all at once. Then, the image of a face rose up in my mind.

Think! Think about the timing.

Addicts steal to support their habits.

Excitement filled me as it all became clear. I knew who was guilty, and I was pretty sure I had a good idea of the motive behind the crimes!

Someone with the initials A. C.

No, it didn't fit. Why didn't it? Everything else was suddenly falling into place nicely, but I couldn't ignore the fact that this detail was at odds with the rest of it.

I sighed in exasperation, dropped my head onto the desk on the verge of tears. It had all seemed so right; how could it be wrong? If only I could *make* it fit.

My eyes flew wide open! I smiled.

For the next forty minutes I made careful notes, writing down everything I knew about the whole situation, and how it all came together to back up my conclusion. When I was finished I was satisfied that I was absolutely correct.

But would the police listen to me? How could I convince them that they should investigate someone else, when they were convinced Amber was guilty? There was nothing solid, no proof to offer them.

How could I get proof? If I was right, the stolen money was almost certainly long gone. And the things taken at school would be too. But where?

I heard my parents' bedroom door open then and hurried to the kitchen, where I plunked down on a chair to wait. Mom appeared a moment later.

"You're up bright and early," she smiled, kissing the top of my head.

"Where could a person sell a stolen watch, Mom?"

"A stolen watch?" She looked startled, which I guess would be most parents' reaction to that sort of question first thing in the morning.

"What's this about then?" Dad asked, joining me at the table.

"I was wondering where a person could sell a stolen watch. It couldn't be to anyone they knew."

"Well, I suppose the most obvious place would be a pawnshop." Dad is so cool.

He'll answer odd questions like that without asking any of his own.

Mom isn't quite that way, though. She grilled me on why I wanted to know such a thing, but I wasn't ready to tell anyone about my theory. Well, at least not my folks. They might go to the police. If they did that, and it got out, my chance of getting proof would be nil.

"I dunno, I was just wondering," I said feebly. Why hadn't I thought of some cover story for the question? But it was all right, because Dad changed the subject and got Mom talking about border for the hallway. How on earth she fell for his diversion I have no idea. After living with him all these years, you'd think she'd know that border would be just about the last thing he'd ever be interested in discussing.

I ate a bowl of cereal and got ready for school as quickly as I could. Wanting to get out of the house before Mom remembered she hadn't actually finished grilling me, I grabbed my jacket and bookbag.

"See you later," I called as I dashed out the door.

I was hoping that Greg might be at school early, but there was no sign of him when I got there. In fact, there was hardly anyone around. The buses started arriving a few moments later and I watched until I saw Laura Peters, the girl whose watch had been stolen, get off one of them.

"Laura! Wait up."

She turned, looking puzzled when she saw me. We're not really friends or anything, so she must have wondered why I'd be calling her.

I hurried over to where she was standing. "Laura, the watch that was stolen from you, what does it look like?"

"Why?" Her face lit up with hope. Ignoring the fact that I obviously didn't even know what it looked like, she then asked, "Have you seen it?"

"No, but I have an idea. Please don't get your hopes up, because it might come to nothing."

"It's a gold Cardinal, with an expansion bracelet and fold-over clasp. The face is oval and there are two diamonds set in it, one at the top and one at the bottom. Do you really think you might be able to find it for me?" She looked wistful. "My grandmother gave that to me before she died you know."

"I know, and I promise that I'll do everything I can to try to find it."

I scribbled down the details she'd given me inside a notebook and then went to my locker. Afterward, I wandered around trying unsuccessfully to find Greg. When the bell rang for first class I had to accept the fact that I wouldn't get a chance to talk to him until lunch.

It was maddening, trying to concentrate on my subjects through the morning. My head was still spinning with excitement, and I was dying to tell Greg about my idea.

Besides, I was going to need his help to get the proof that would make the police reopen the investigation.

CHAPTER TWENTY-SEVEN

By lunchtime my stomach was all tied up in nervous knots from waiting to talk to Greg. I slid into my seat at our usual table, doubtful if I could force down a single bite of my tuna on whole wheat, even though it's my favourite kind of sandwich.

It was then that I realized I'd never be able to discuss the whole thing with him when there were so many other students nearby. If anyone overheard, my idea could be seriously jeopardized.

"As soon as you're finished eating," I whispered, leaning forward, "I want to go somewhere that we can talk privately.

"With Amber?"

"No, I need to talk to you alone."

"Well, we can't very well leave her by herself."

I hadn't thought of that. My frustration rose, but

there wasn't much I could do about it. Greg was right, there was no way we could abandon her at the one time during the school day she could spend time with friendly faces.

Amber was a few minutes late arriving for lunch. I figured she'd waited for the halls to clear a bit before making her way to the cafeteria. She shuffled in, head down, and made her way to the table without once looking up. I couldn't help thinking that made her look guilty, as if she was ashamed and couldn't face anyone. On the other hand, I don't think I'd have had the courage to keep my head up either, if I'd been in her position.

We started chatting, avoiding the subject of the robberies as if we'd agreed to set it aside for the time being. Part of me wanted to let Amber in on my theory, but it seemed too risky. She was the one with the most to lose and she might be tempted to let something slip that would help clear her name. It was imperative that the real culprit had no warning. That could provide either time or opportunity to cover up clues.

I was facing the entrance of the cafeteria, and a few minutes after Amber had joined us, I noticed a stranger come into the room. It was a tall man, thin, with dark hair and eyes. Although I knew I'd never seen him before there was something familiar about him.

He stopped after taking a few steps inside the entrance and began scanning the crowded room, obviously searching for someone. With a jolt, I realized what was familiar about him.

"Amber," I could hardly get my voice to work, "I think your dad is here."

"*What?*" Comprehension came slowly, and then her head spun around and she saw him. Rising shakily to her feet she half stumbled and half ran across the room. His face lit up as he saw her coming, and before she'd reached him his arms had opened to catch her. She flew into them and he clasped her against his chest, holding her tight.

"How'd you know that was her father?" Greg asked.

"Can't you see the resemblance?" I asked, and when he admitted that he couldn't I didn't hold it against him. After all, guys aren't very good at that sort of thing.

"Well, it looks as though we'll have a chance to talk after all," Greg eyed my untouched lunch. "Aren't you going to eat?"

"I can't. My stomach is all nervous and excited." While everyone's attention was firmly riveted on Amber and her father, I took the opportunity to whisper, "I think I know who did it."

"I knew you'd get it!" His face broke into a wide grin. "Let's go talk then."

We cleared our table and headed outside. By then, Amber and her father had also gone out. Reaching the parking lot we saw the two of them talking animatedly beside a car. Amber was laughing and crying all at the same time, her arms waving in bird-like flutters while her father seemed to be fighting his own tears.

"That's the best thing that's happened to her since she got here," Greg commented as we observed them for a moment. "It will give her the lift she needs. And of course, now that you've solved the crimes, her problems in Little River are all but over."

"I hope so. The thing is, I'm almost positive I know who did it, but there's no proof. I have to get some solid evidence before I can go to the police. I'm going to need your help."

"You've got it. Now, tell me everything."

"Okay, here's the thing. You know all the clues that didn't seem to make sense? They came together when I realized that some of them weren't exactly about the culprit."

He looked puzzled and I continued. "The part about mothers protecting their children suddenly made sense when I put it together with what that horrid woman at the convenience store said about reputation and not everything being about money."

"I'm not following you."

"Remember when Broderick's was robbed and a reward was offered?"

"Five hundred dollars, yeah."

"Mrs. Carter went to the police and gave them a story about seeing Amber sneaking through someone's yard with a bag in her hands when she was supposed to be at the gas station that night. It looked as though she'd done it for the reward money."

"And she had another reason?"

"Mothers will do anything to protect their children! That's what she was doing. Somehow she either knew or suspected that her son was the thief. She was protecting him."

"Tony?"

"Yes. And the timing. It didn't seem to mean anything until I thought about the fact that one crime was committed at the end of a weekend, and the other happened just before the weekend."

"So, what does that mean?"

"This is my theory. Almost every weekend, Tony goes over to Veander, where his brother is in college. The real question is *why*. Is he that close to his brother that he wants to spend all this time with him, or is there another reason?"

"What kind of reason?"

"Think about what you know about Tony. What's the one thing that he's most known for?"

"His card tricks?"

"Exactly! How does he get it right every time?"

"A marked deck!" Greg looked excited.

"It has to be. There's no way he can correctly guess a card that's face down every time. And why would anyone have a marked deck?"

"For gambling!"

"You've got it." I drew a deep breath. "That's what the idea of an addict meant. It's not about drugs, he's addicted to gambling. I think he's going over to Veander to play poker with the college students."

An image flashed in my mind then, of Tony sitting on the bench in town.

"Oh! I just realized something else! The day before Broderick's was robbed, I saw Tony in the town square. He didn't look quite right, and I thought he was sick or something. He'd been in Veander that weekend, and he told me he got bored and came home early."

"Well, he'd have been home Sunday in any case, wouldn't he?" Greg asked. "So, either way, he'd have been here when Broderick's was robbed."

"Yes, but that's not the point. It wasn't long after lunch when I saw him. The bus doesn't come in until around suppertime."

"So he got back some other way. But why, when he had a bus ticket?"

"That's the thing. As I said, he seemed out of sorts. I think what must have happened was he got into a mess, lost a lot of money that he didn't have or something. He must have had to get out of there fast and then couldn't go to his house until the bus would normally be arriving. That would explain why he was all shook up, and sitting in the town square. And Broderick's was robbed the next day. He must have been desperate to get money to pay back his debt."

"But if he has a marked deck, wouldn't you think he'd win all the time?"

"Do you think they let him use his own deck of cards? These are older guys, they wouldn't be that stupid, especially if he used them a few times and won consistently. But if he's addicted, he can't stop, even if he knows he doesn't have the advantage of cheating like that."

Greg whistled low. "It makes sense. So, how do you prove it?"

"We've got to go to Veander on Saturday. There's a pawnshop over there."

"A pawnshop? What does that have to do with catching him gambling?"

"Nothing, but the things that went missing at school had to be sold somewhere. I guess that's the most likely place to look. He couldn't sell the stuff around here, but no one would know him there. I got a description of the watch that was stolen from Laura. We need to see if we can find it, and a pawnshop in Veander is the most logical place to look."

"Wait a minute, Shelby. I just thought of something. What about the key chain? The initials on it are A. C. Tony's initials are T. C."

"That's something that almost completely threw me off," I admitted.

"So how do you explain it?"

"Tony is a derivative," I smiled, "of Anthony!"

CHAPTER TWENTY-EIGHT

"You're a genius!"

I blushed at the compliment, which I suppose modesty should at least have made me insist was an overstatement. But I *was* feeling pretty smart at the moment, and anyway, if Greg wanted to call me a genius, it would have been rude to argue.

"Tony is a form of Anthony," he pondered. "Of course! I never would have thought of that."

"And his grandparents might refer to him by his proper name," I added. "Lots of older people do that."

"Especially if he was named after a relative." Greg hugged me impulsively.

We were so engrossed in our conversation that we didn't notice Amber and her father approaching us. They had almost reached the spot we were standing when I happened to glance up and see them there. Both wore enormous smiles.

"Dad, these are my friends, Shelby and Greg."

Mr. Chapman shook our hands and we all said we were happy to meet each other. He told us he appreciated how kind we'd been to his daughter, standing by her when things were so rough.

"Amber should have told me the problems she was having," he sighed. "I knew nothing about it until I got a call from the police. Of course, as soon as I heard, I made arrangements to get here as quickly as I could."

"How long will you be staying?" Greg asked.

"As long as it takes to get this cleared up." His eyes were misting over. "And then I'm letting my company know that I either get a permanent assignment in Canada or I'm looking for another job."

"I'm going to be living with my dad, as soon as he gets settled back in Canada." Amber's face was glowing with happiness.

"Sometimes a man needs a thing like this to happen," Mr. Chapman said somberly. "It sure opened my eyes about what's important."

"It just goes to show," Greg commented to me after Amber and her dad had left, "that even the worst situations can bring something good."

I agreed with him on that. Who knows if Mr. Chapman would ever have made the decision to have his daughter live with him, if the whole robbery thing hadn't occurred? I was really happy and excited that life was changing for the better for Amber. It seemed to make up for everything she'd had to go through first.

The bell was ringing for afternoon classes then, and we didn't have time to talk anymore about arrangements to get to Veander. Greg promised he'd come over after dinner so we could make plans.

He arrived just as I'd finished sweeping the kitchen floor, and we went off to my room to talk in privacy.

"Keep your door open a bit," Mom admonished as we headed down the hallway. I blushed at that, because it sounded as if she didn't trust us.

"Sorry about that," I whispered to Greg, wondering if he felt insulted.

"What, about having the door open?" he whispered back. "Don't apologize for that. Anyway, I was kind of worried you might try to take advantage of me."

"Yeah, you wish." I swatted his arm, giggling.

"Oh, I know what you girls are like. You get a guy alone and use him for your own twisted purposes, then you tell all your friends how easy he was."

It was the closest we'd ever come to talking about that sort of thing, and even though he was joking, I wondered what he really thought about it. I expected the subject of sex would come up sometime and didn't know how I'd handle it. Greg is like my ideal guy and I'm crazy about him, but this was my first real relationship, and I knew I wasn't ready to jump into anything like that.

For all that Mom sometimes drives me crazy with her endless talks, I was glad we'd discussed this. She'd made me think hard about how the choices you make when you're young can affect you all your life.

"Just make sure you don't do anything that you might end up regretting later," she'd told me. That had surprised me. I would have thought she'd have said something more dramatic or tried to frighten me with talk of disease and the like. The fact that her whole talk had focused on me and my feelings had sunk in more than any scare tactics would have.

I pushed those thoughts aside and made myself think about Veander.

"Do you think you can get this Saturday off work?" I asked.

"I'll ask. I think Mr. Broderick will give it to me, though. He's really reasonable and I've never asked for a day off before. In fact, why don't I call him right now? There's not much sense in making plans until we know for sure."

Unlike Betts, I have no phone in my room, though I've hinted for one a few times. Well, maybe "hinted" isn't the right word. I guess the truth is that I've pestered my folks about it, but so far they haven't given in. Greg went to the kitchen to make his call and came back after a few moments.

"No problem."

"Great! Now, the next question. How do we get there?"

"What about the bus?"

"No good. I checked the schedule the other day. We wouldn't have time to get there, do what we have to do, and come back the same day."

"Well, I haven't had my license very long, so I can guarantee my dad's not going to give me the car for the day. Especially not for a trip out of town. What about the train?"

"I hadn't even thought of the train. But you know, that should work. It leaves here around nine in the morning. That would give us time to check things and get the bus back in the afternoon." I took a deep breath. "There's another problem though."

"What's that?"

"Money. I haven't saved much from my allowances or what I've earned babysitting. And I'm not allowed to touch my bank account because Mom makes the deposits in that and it's for university."

"Well, that's the least of our worries," he said without hesitating. "I can take care of the cost of the tickets. But are you sure you can get away for the day? I take it that you're not planning to tell your parents what you're up to."

"No way! They'd have a conniption. I'd never be allowed to go."

"I have to admit that I'm not wild about deceiving your mom and dad, but I understand you feel there's no choice. You *do* realize they're going to have to know about it at some point, don't you?"

"I know, but I figure by then it will be over with and there won't be much they can do about it. Well, except maybe ground me for a couple of years or so."

"They might also decide you shouldn't be hanging around with me, since I'll be involved in the whole thing."

I hadn't considered that. Even though I was almost sure they wouldn't actually forbid me from seeing Greg, it would probably change their opinion of him. That was the last thing I wanted to see happen.

Seeing the alarmed expression on my face, Greg said, "It's your call, Shelby. I'll go along with your decision."

I sighed. There wasn't going to be an easy solution, but Amber was our friend and we had to help her.

"It'll all work out okay." I tried to sound more confident than I felt. "Anyway, we'll worry about the repercussions later."

In the meantime, I was going to have to come up with a story that would get me out of the house for the whole day on Saturday.

CHAPTER TWENTY-NINE

It was easier than I'd expected. When I told Mom and Dad that I was spending the day with Greg on Saturday, they accepted it without asking for details. That was a huge relief to me, because even though I'd prepared a story about us going hiking and taking a picnic lunch, I know I'd never have carried it off. I'd have sputtered and stammered and turned red, the way I always do when I try to tell something that's not true.

We met at the train station about half an hour before it was to leave and Greg bought our tickets, dismissing my promise to pay him back when I could.

"You did all the sleuthing," he said simply. "This is the least I can do. It makes me feel good to think I'm helping Amber in some small way."

There were few passengers on board that morning, and the car we sat in had only four other occupants. Three were together, a mother and her two small children, while the other was an elderly man who kept frowning and muttering about the noise the little ones made.

"They're just kids," I whispered to Greg, "You'd think he could be a bit more tolerant."

"Maybe he's tired or ill. Or maybe he's lonely and depressed because his wife just died and this is his first time travelling without her."

"Well, he could move to another car if he wanted to. I say he's just a nasty old man who hates children and loves complaining," I sighed, feigning exasperation. "Do you have to be so insufferably nice all the time?"

"Sorry, I'll work on that." He forced the smile from his face and glowered at me. "I know. I'll practise on you."

"Go away!" I giggled at his stern look, which was exaggerated to the point of being ridiculous. "You couldn't do it if you tried."

"I could if you weren't so darned cute." He kissed the tip of my nose, which was thankfully zit-free at the moment.

We were in Veander before we knew it, and my stomach started doing excited flip-flops as soon as we got off the train. The station was just on the outskirts of town but we took a cab so as not to lose any time walking, asking the driver to let us off at the pawnshop.

It was a musty, dusty-looking store, too small for its contents. There were things stacked and piled everywhere, and it seemed that little attention had been paid to creating any kind of order. The walls were covered with pegboards, and every square inch was cluttered with everything from guitars to porcelain dolls.

I figured the man behind the counter to be the owner, since he watched us with some suspicion from the second we walked inside. He was probably in his fifties, short and chubby with pasty skin that apparently saw little sunlight.

"Yep?" he asked, which I assumed was his way of asking if he could help us.

"Yes, good morning," Greg nodded to him. "We'd like to see your jewelry."

"Kinda jewelry?" Apparently small talk was not this man's strong point.

"Oh, rings, watches, necklaces. Shelby here isn't quite sure what she'd like. You know how women are."

The only reply to this was a grunt, but the man shuffled over to the end wall, lifted a large black case from its resting place beside a rocking chair, and lugged it to the counter.

The inside of the case was surprisingly organized. Once opened, we could see that it contained five separate trays, each holding assorted pieces of jewelry.

I pretended to be interested in several of the items as I looked through, scanning each tray carefully for a watch that matched the description Laura had given. My heart sank when I saw that it wasn't there.

"I don't know, I was really hoping for a watch, but I don't see anything here that's quite what I wanted."

"Kinda watch?" The thought of making a sale prompted our taciturn helper to summon his voice again.

"Well, something a little fancier than the ones here. Gold, maybe."

Greg smiled and shrugged. "What can I say. The lady has expensive taste. Would you have anything else?"

His reaction startled us when he turned and walked away without a word. We looked at each other questioningly, wondering what he was up to, but then saw that he was talking to someone on an intercom.

"Joe, got any gold watches?"

"Say what?"

"Watches, gold watches. Got any?"

"Just a sec."

A moment later a younger and slightly thinner version of the older man appeared from a back entrance. The similarity of what was clearly father and son ended there, though.

"Hey, how are ya? Great day isn't it? Looking for a watch for the little woman, are we? Have you checked our selection out here? Yes, I see you have. Well, what did you have in mind, exactly?"

"I'd like a dressy watch, something in gold if you have it."

"Gold, huh? Well, we might have two or three in our holding room, but they won't be for sale until the redemption time is up. If the owners don't come back for them, that is."

"Would it be possible to see them anyway?" Greg asked. "Then if she likes one, we could check back when it might be available."

"I don't suppose there'd be any harm in looking," he winked at me. "Be right back."

He was gone and back in a flash, holding four small brown envelopes. I knew we'd found what we were looking for before I even saw the third one. The envelope's flap was labelled, in black marker.

It said T. Carter.

I held out my hand as Joe drew out the watch and passed it to me. It fit Laura's description perfectly.

"I love this one," I said, trying to keep my voice from trembling with the excitement I felt. "How much is it?"

"That one's seventy-five dollars. Those are real diamonds though; it's well worth the price. It's in hock for another, let's see, thirty days or so. But I think you're safe with it. Young fellow brings things in all the time. Never comes back for any of it."

"We could come back in a month," I said to Greg, "And get it then."

"Don't leave it too long," Joe studied the flap. "It'll be out for sale after the second of June. Good watches don't hang around, so if you want it be sure to come in around that time."

We thanked him, said goodbye to the pair, and left the store. Neither of us spoke or reacted until we had gone down the street and turned the corner. Then we whooped and did high fives and hugged.

With the rest of the day to kill, we window-shopped and had lunch at a sweet little café where the tables were covered with checkered cloths. The food was only average, but the ambience made up for it, with old-fashioned décor and a waitress dressed in a long, peasant-style skirt and a white blouse.

The bus ride home went quickly, and I was glad to be back in Little River. The next step was deciding what to do with the information I now had that would save Amber.

I thought the house was empty when I first got home, since the car wasn't in the driveway. When I walked past the living room, though, I saw Dad sitting in his easy chair, reading the paper. He put it aside when he saw me and beckoned me into the room.

"So, Shelby," he asked in a tone that was just a little *too* casual. "Would you like to tell me what you were up to today?"

CHAPTER THIRTY

"I was with Greg," I answered Dad's question with a sinking heart. "I thought I told you and Mom that he and I had plans today."

"So you did." He looked serious. "In fact, you mentioned it more than once. Three or four times, if I'm not mistaken. Bit of overkill, wouldn't you say?"

"What do you mean?" I could feel my face getting warm and tried to take deep, even breaths to calm myself. Turning red wouldn't do anything to help me look innocent.

"I mean that I know my daughter well enough to see when she's up to something. Want to tell me about it?"

I didn't. Not at all. But it wasn't as if I had a choice. Somehow, I'd given myself away, though I can never understand out how parents figure these things out. It's like they have some kind of radar, sort of like the way dogs hear sounds no one else can hear.

I sank down onto the couch and faced him, though it was pretty hard to look him in the eye. And I told him the whole story, from start to finish. He didn't interrupt.

"So you went to Veander."

"Yes."

"Bit of a waste of money, wasn't it?"

"I *had* to go." Hadn't he heard me explain how we'd found the watch, the evidence that would help to clear Amber's name?

"Well, yes, I can see that. But I'd have driven you over if you'd asked."

"You *would* have?"

"Sure."

"You'd have let me go? And not said anything to the police first?"

"Listen, munchkin, I have no problem with what you did. None. Only with the way you went about it, being sneaky and all. You tend to make these assumptions about your mother and I that end up backfiring on you. If you'd told us the truth right from the start, we'd have done anything we could to help."

"I didn't know ..." I trailed off, searching for words, feeling ashamed. "I thought if I told you what was going on ..."

"We'd have mucked it all up somehow?"

"I guess." I figure I was about the same shade of red as a checker piece by then. "I'm sorry, Dad."

"Well, now, nothing to be sorry about." He reached across and patted my arm, which almost made me cry. "You're a great girl and your mother and I are always proud of you.

"You did a wonderful thing, solving this robbery business and helping your friend. And I'm not trying to take away any of the thrill that must give you. I just want you to see that you can trust us. With anything."

I did cry then, but I'm not exactly sure why since I wasn't in trouble after all. It seemed that Dad being so understanding and nice about it somehow made me feel worse than if he'd grounded me.

When I'd gotten myself under control, dried my tears, and blown my nose, I asked Dad what he thought I should do next. I explained my one remaining worry.

"I'm a bit afraid the police might not listen to me, seeing as I'm just a kid. Especially since they had the crazy idea I might have been involved."

"Sadly enough, you could be right."

"The worst thing is that they might resent the fact that they made a mistake in arresting Amber for the robberies. And the watch at the pawnshop doesn't prove Tony committed those, just the thefts at school. They might dismiss what I tell them as not being related."

He nodded but didn't make any suggestions or offer to help. It occurred to me that he could be waiting for me to ask first.

"Will you go with me? To the police station? They'd listen to you."

"Of course I will. Be glad to." His face told me I'd been right, he'd been hoping I'd ask him to go along. "Your mother should be home shortly. We'll go then."

Mom did indeed arrive not long after that, but there was a delay while Dad filled her in on everything before we left for the police station. He made it easy on me (not that I deserved it) by talking to her himself while I stayed in my room feeling cowardly. He must have done a good job smoothing things over, because she didn't seem cross when I finally emerged and faced her.

When we got to the police station Dad asked to speak to the desk sergeant, and a moment later an officer came along.

"Can I help you, sir?"

"You can. My daughter here, Shelby, has some important information related to the recent robberies in Little River."

We were ushered into an interview room right away and the officer sat down with us, leaning forward to listen.

I explained about the thefts at school, and how the robberies had started when everyone began to take precautions to prevent anything further being stolen from lockers and so on.

"You should have at least one of these on file," I added. "Laura Peters's watch was stolen first, and I'm pretty sure she reported it to the police."

"Yes, I recall seeing that file." He nodded encouragingly. I got the feeling he was waiting for me to say something incriminating about Amber.

I went on and told him about how I'd become suspicious of one of the students and detailed the various things that had happened. Then I told him about the trip to the pawnshop and how the stolen watch was there. It wasn't until I mentioned Tony Carter that his expression changed.

"Our suspect is another individual," he commented, as though everyone in town didn't already know that.

"But she didn't do it. Tony did."

"Well, I'm sure you mean to help." His voice was condescending, which really annoyed me. "But there's no reason to think the stolen watch has any connection to the robberies. One is petty theft, the other armed robbery. There's quite a difference."

Then his tone turned downright dismissive and he told us he appreciated us coming and he'd look into the matter of the watch.

"Aren't you even going to check it out?" I know I sounded desperate, which was how I felt at the moment.

It looked as if everything I'd done was for nothing.

"We'll question the youth," he said in a way that made me feel I was being humoured.

"What about the key?"

"What about it?"

"Aren't you going to see if it fits the Carters' door?" I explained about the initials on the key chain and how they fit Tony as well as Amber.

"We'll look into it." His voice was unconvinced, and he seemed tired and disinterested. I was furious.

"I certainly hope you'll investigate this thoroughly," Dad spoke for the first time since the interview had begun. His tone was firm and almost angry. He looked as if he was going to add something bordering on a threat, probably about the press, but before he could go on, I thought of something else.

"Remember how Mrs. Carter gave a statement about seeing Amber the night of the gas station robbery?" I blurted, not ready to accept defeat. "Why would she have done that, unless she was trying to protect her son?"

That was the turning point. Though his expression didn't change, I could see something in the officer's eyes that told me he was finally interested in my theory.

"We *will* look into it," he said in a new tone. Relief washed over me. I knew that he meant it this time and that he'd keep his word.

CHAPTER THIRTY-ONE

"Oh, Shelby!" Amber's voice was breathless and happy. "It's over. The police have dropped the charges against me."

After all the anxiety and mental strain of the past weeks I actually felt myself sag with relief at the announcement. It was as if all the energy had drained out of me.

"That's great, Amber!" was all I could think to say.

"I guess they found out who really did it and have already made another arrest. And I thought they weren't even looking for anyone else."

I could have told her that I was the one who'd solved the crime and gone to the police. But I didn't. It might have sounded as if I was bragging or looking for thanks from her. The truth was that since the day I'd tricked her into picking up my watch in the girls' room at school, I'd felt I owed her something. Now I could stop feeling guilty about that.

The very next day I had a surprise phone call from the desk sergeant I'd spoken to about Tony.

"Miss Belgarden," his voice boomed in the receiver, "I want to congratulate you on a fine piece of detective work. I checked out the lead you gave us and you were right on."

"So the key fit the Carters' door?" I asked.

"Nope, we tried both doors, but it didn't work in either."

"Then how …?"

"I was convinced you were on to something. What you said about his mother protecting him made me keep looking. So I started calling locksmiths and found out that Mrs. Carter had the lock to the front door replaced a few weeks ago. The locksmith who'd taken out the old set had kept it, since it still worked just fine. The key fit that lock."

"Wow! That was pretty smart," I blurted, realizing too late that the surprised tone of my voice might be insulting. But the officer only laughed.

"Well, thanks. Actually, we should have picked up on that earlier. Any experienced officer knows that things that don't fit are often important pieces of evidence. We should have realized that something was up when Mrs. Carter made the false report. She's not a crank who does that sort of thing. But we were caught up in investigating Miss Chapman, and missed it."

"I was worried that you were so sure Amber was guilty you might not check out my story," I confessed.

"Heck, we're just as capable of making mistakes as anyone else," he replied. "But we're willing to admit when we're wrong."

I'd been pretty disgusted with the police before talking to the sergeant, but afterward I had a whole new opinion. I realized they'd done what anyone would do with the information they had. It was true that it had all seemed to point toward Amber.

And of course I'd been in a position to see things they couldn't — because I was around Tony. They didn't know about his "lucky" deck of cards, or his weekends in Veander, or the other things that had led me to the conclusion I'd reached. If they'd missed the clue about his mother, it was the only thing they'd overlooked.

Greg's prediction about what would happen at school turned out to be absolutely correct. Everyone was enormously embarrassed for the way they'd treated us and went out of their way to make amends. Amber was suddenly swamped with people wanting to be friends with her. Only this time she accepted friendly overtures graciously, and before long it seemed she was the most popular student at Little River High. There were even a few other girls who started wearing unusual outfits, trying to copy her unique style.

Betts was almost shy when she first came back to sit at our table at lunch, which, if you know Betts, is highly out of character. I could see that she was uncomfortable and maybe a little ashamed for not sticking with us when things got rough. But there have been lots of times when Betts has been there for me when I was down or having some sort of problem, and remembering that helped me get past any resentment I might have felt over her bailing on us this time. In no time things were back to normal and we were hanging out at each other's places as usual.

Amber (and everyone else) found out about my involvement in solving the crime because of Greg, even though I'd asked him not to say anything. She and her father showed up at our door one evening, and once they'd come in and been introduced to my parents, Amber drew me aside to speak privately for a moment.

"Greg filled me in on everything you did," she said softly. "You know, I feel so bad when I think of the way I acted the first day we met. I was just so unhappy at the time that I was horrid to you."

"It's okay." I hugged her, remembering how lost and sad she'd been. "I understand. Anyway, it all turned out okay and that's what matters."

"I can never tell you how much I appreciate what you did for my daughter," her father told me. He was all misty-eyed and choked up, which made me feel like crying myself, though that would have been dumb. He shook my hand solemnly and told my parents what a fine young woman I was to have helped someone I barely knew.

"You must have done a great job raising her," he added, and there was pain in his voice. I figured he was thinking with regret about his own daughter and how she'd taken second place to her mother's new husband and to her father's job. I was glad his eyes had been opened and he was going to change things for her.

Then he told us that his company had agreed to give him a permanent job in Mississauga and that Amber would be going to live with him once the school year ended. I was really happy for her.

When they were leaving, he gave me a large manila envelope. I opened it after they were gone and saw that it held a thank-you card and another large envelope. The card read:

> *Once in a long while in this journey we call life (and only if we are very, very lucky) we encounter those rare individuals whose self-less actions make our world a better place. You are such a person. It will give us great*

*pleasure if you will accept this small token
of our appreciation and esteem.*

Curious, I drew a single sheet from the other envelope, then gasped as I saw that it was a certificate bearing my name. What he'd referred to as a "small token" was a scholarship fund in the amount of ten thousand dollars!

"Mom, Dad," I could barely speak as I held it out for them to see. For a moment we all stared at the certificate, too stunned to react.

"I guess I can't keep this," I sighed, certain that's what they'd say. But I was wrong.

"Well, now, I think it would be insulting to try to return it," Dad said. "Mr. Chapman is obviously a man of some means, and I don't suppose he'd have given this to you if he couldn't well afford it. He's probably only too happy to be able to do something for you, in return for what you did for Amber. It's a huge gift, but I don't see any reason you can't have it."

Mom agreed, though she did her usual thing of saying I should write a nice letter thanking Mr. Chapman for the generous gift, as if I wouldn't have known enough to do that without her telling me.

Ten thousand dollars towards my education! I was overwhelmed. It seemed such an enormous amount, and I certainly hadn't expected to get anything. But then, that might be part of the joy Mr. Chapman would have gotten in giving it — knowing that it would come as a complete surprise.

The one person I felt most sorry for in the end was, believe it or not, Tony. I expected him to despise me once he found out I was the one who'd gone to the police about him, but I soon discovered that wasn't true. He came to my locker one morning, which kind of scared me. I was sure he was going to say something nasty. What he did say was entirely different.

"I guess you must hate me."

"Hate you?" Surprise showed in my tone. "Why?"

"Because your friend almost got blamed for what I did."

"That's true," I conceded, "but I don't hate you for it. I know you were in a mess, and it would have been pretty hard to go to the police and confess."

"I should have, though. It got so I couldn't even sleep at night. I kept thinking about that poor girl and how she was being accused for something I'd done. On top of it, I had all these gambling debts that I couldn't pay, and the more I tried to win back the money, the deeper in debt I got. It was like a sickness."

"It must have been awful for you."

"My stomach was so nauseated most of the time that I could hardly even eat. It was like living in one of those dreams where you're trying to run from something and your feet are moving but you're not going anywhere and the thing chasing you keeps getting closer and closer. Know what I mean?"

I nodded.

"I was scared all the time. Scared of what was going to happen to me if I couldn't keep coming up with the money I owed. Scared of being found out. And still, I couldn't stop. Now, even though everyone knows what I did and I have to go to court, it's like a huge weight off me. I'll never gamble again."

"Everyone makes mistakes, Tony. I hope things will get better for you now."

"They already are. It's like I finally got away from the thing that was going to catch me. And you know what the worst thing is? It's knowing that my mother saw what was going on all along and never did anything about it. If it wasn't for you, I'd still be gambling and stealing, getting in deeper and deeper. I owe you."

I didn't argue with that. I guess it was better for him to feel he owed me something than to owe gambling debts.

ACKNOWLEDGEMENTS

The muse and I acknowledge, with thanks, contributions from the following persons:

My husband, partner, and best friend, Brent, for his endless love, faith, and support.

My children, Anthony and Pamela, for inspiring me daily.

My parents, Bob and Pauline Russell, and my brothers, Danny and Andrew, and their respective partners, Gail and Shelley, for their love and encouragement.

The Sherrards, for being my second family in every sense.

My sixth grade teacher, Alf Lower, for planting the seed that grew.

Friends who have been amazingly supportive are: Janet Aube, Karen Donovan, Ray Doucet, Karen Dyer, John Hambrook, Sandra Henderson, Marsha Skrypuch, and Bonnie Thompson. At work, I have been much encouraged by my exceptional staff: Jimmy Allain, Karen Arseneault, Carol Forrest, Mary Matchett, Julia Trevors, Ann Craik, Beatrice Tucker, Dawn Black, Gabrielle Kennedy, Sharon Murphy, Sue Fitzpatrick, Eric Fallon, Edison Jardine, and Dianne Miles.

At The Dundurn Group, I am sincerely grateful to Kirk Howard, Publisher, and the team that makes the complicated task of turning out a final product look easy. Particular thanks are due to:

Barry Jowett, Senior Editor, for his guidance, support, and patience.

Kerry Breeze, who was a great publicist and is a grand human being.

Andrea Pruss, Copy Editor, for knowing all the rules.

Jennifer Scott, for her amazing cover designs.

Jennifer Easter (Queen Jen) for innumerable behind-the-scenes efforts.